Wuthering Heights

First published in 2003 by Usborne Publishing Ltd,
Usborne House, 83-85 Saffron Hill,
London EC1N 8RT, England.
www.usborne.com

A catalogue record for this title is available
from the British Library.

ISBN 07460 5750 4

Printed in Great Britain

Designed by Sarah Cronin
Series editors: Jane Chisholm and Rosie Dickins
Series designer: Mary Cartwright
Cover photograph © Matthew Hollerbush/CORBIS
Cover design by Glen Bird
With thanks to Georgina Andrews

Wuthering Heights

From the story by Emily Brontë

Retold by Jane Bingham

Illustrated by Darrell Warner

Contents

Introduction

When *Wuthering Heights* was first published in 1847, many people were shocked by its passion and violence. The book's dramatic scenes, set against the wild Yorkshire moors, made it very different from most Victorian novels. Some people imagined that its author, Ellis Bell, must be a very strange man, but in fact Ellis Bell was the pen name of a young woman.

Born in 1818, Emily Brontë was the fifth child of the Reverend Patrick Brontë, rector of Haworth church in Yorkshire, northern England. She lived almost all her life in Haworth Parsonage, a small stone house surrounded by miles of rugged, open moorland.

Young Emily had many happy times playing with her brother and sisters, and walking and riding on the moors, but she also had some sad experiences. When she was only three years old, her mother died of cancer. At the age of six, she was sent with her sister Charlotte to join their two older sisters at Cowan Bridge boarding school for girls. The teachers at Cowan Bridge were extremely strict, the school was freezing cold in winter and unbearably hot in summer, and the girls did not have enough to eat. Within six months, tuberculosis – a serious lung disease – had swept through the school, killing the two older Brontë girls.

After this, Emily and Charlotte were sent back home again, where they spent the rest of their childhood at Haworth, with their older brother Branwell and their younger sister Anne. The four Brontë children led very isolated lives, but they were all very imaginative and they amused themselves by creating fantasy lands partly inspired by Branwell's set of toy soldiers. Charlotte and Branwell invented the land of Angria, while Emily and Anne created the kingdom of Gondal. They made up characters to live in their imaginary countries and wrote down all their adventures in tiny notebooks.

Emily was an intelligent, lively child who became quieter and more withdrawn as she grew older. She loved to lie in front of the fire reading, and was very fond of animals. Emily could also be adventurous and brave. She learned to use her father's pistol, and once, when she was bitten by a dog, she held a red-hot poker to the wound to stop it from bleeding.

Apart from a few months away from home, Emily spent all her adult life at Haworth, looking after her father and brother. At first she was happy, but life at the Parsonage became more and more difficult. The Brontës were not rich and Branwell was a wreck. He had not lived up to his early promise as a writer and a painter, and had become addicted to alcohol and opium. But, despite her troubles, Emily kept writing stories and poems.

In 1846, when Emily was 27, Charlotte persuaded Emily and Anne to publish a joint collection of poems under the pen names of Currer, Ellis and Acton Bell. The following year, Currer Bell (Charlotte Brontë) published the novel *Jane Eyre*, while Ellis Bell (Emily) published *Wuthering Heights*. Although Charlotte's novel was an immediate success, the critics were much less positive about *Wuthering Heights*.

In 1848, Branwell Brontë died of tuberculosis, and Emily caught a bad cold at his funeral. She refused to see a doctor and continued to care for her father and run the family home. Emily died two months later, in December 1848, at the age of 30. Charlotte described her sister's last few months in her introduction to the 1850 edition of *Wuthering Heights*: "Day by day, when I saw with what a front she met suffering, I looked on her with anguish of wonder and love. I have seen nothing like it; but, indeed, I have never seen her parallel in anything. Stronger than a man, simpler than a child, her nature stood alone."

Emily Brontë was an adventurous storyteller. Instead of starting at the beginning of the story, the first scene of *Wuthering Heights* plunges into a time close to the end. Later, there is a long flashback when we learn what has happened up until then and, finally, the last part of the story is told. She also uses different narrators, or storytellers. The first narrator is an outsider, Charles Lockwood, who visits Wuthering Heights without knowing about its past. He is very confused about what is going on, which adds to the novel's sense of mystery. The second narrator, Nelly Dean, is the housekeeper who grew up with the novel's two main characters – Cathy and Heathcliff. She describes the events she has seen, but parts of her story are told by other characters. At the end of the novel, Charles Lockwood returns to Wuthering Heights and tells the last part of the story.

Wuthering Heights is full of deliberate contrasts. The bleak farmhouse of Wuthering Heights, high up on the moors, is contrasted with the comfortable Thrushcross Grange, safe in the valley, while the passionate, dark-haired Earnshaws are set against the gentle, fair-haired Lintons. The action shifts between Wuthering Heights and Thrushcross Grange as the two families meet and react to each other.

With many bitter experiences of death and illness, Emily Brontë didn't have an easy life, but she was also passionately happy on her beloved moors. All these experiences are reflected in her novel. Like its author's life, *Wuthering Heights* contains some very sad events, and many of its characters die young. It is also filled with vivid descriptions of nature and weather, and some of its most dramatic scenes take place on the moors. Cathy and Heathcliff are both closely identified with the moors and nature, and Heathcliff is compared to a rocky crag, a greedy cuckoo and a prowling wolf. The bleak farmhouse in *Wuthering Heights* may have been based on a real house that Emily Brontë knew, or she may have drawn on details of her own family home to create the house that gives her book its name. Some literary critics have suggested that the character of Cathy is very like Emily Brontë herself, while Heathcliff may represent the sort of man Emily could have loved.

Charlotte Brontë described her sister creating the story of *Wuthering Heights* as if she were carving a sculpture out of rock, "the crag took human shape, and there it stands colossal, dark and frowning, half statue, half rock." Some people find the novel dark and frightening, but its haunting sense of mystery has helped to make it one of the world's most famous stories of love and revenge.

Family Tree

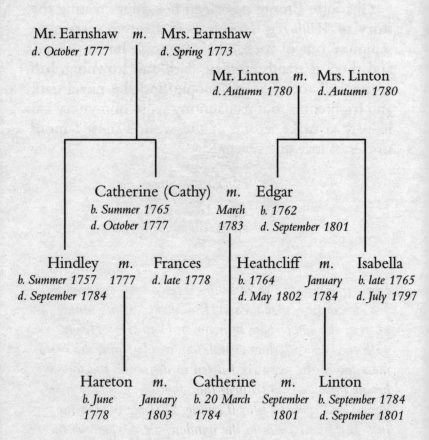

Mr. Earnshaw *m.* Mrs. Earnshaw
d. October 1777   *d. Spring 1773*

Mr. Linton *m.* Mrs. Linton
d. Autumn 1780   *d. Autumn 1780*

Catherine (Cathy) *m.* Edgar
b. Summer 1765   *March*   *b. 1762*
d. October 1777   *1783*   *d. September 1801*

Hindley *m.* Frances
b. Summer 1757 *1777* *d. late 1778*
d. September 1784

Heathcliff *m.* Isabella
b. 1764   *January* *b. late 1765*
d. May 1802 *1784* *d. July 1797*

Hareton *m.* Catherine *m.* Linton
b. June   *January*   *b. 20 March* *September* *b. September 1784*
1778   *1803*   *1784*   *1801*   *d. Septmber 1801*

A face at the window

Ever since my stay in Yorkshire, I have been troubled by bad dreams. In these dreams, I'm always in the same place… the small, bare bedroom at Wuthering Heights, with the snow swirling outside the window and the wind moaning in the trees. As I listen to the wind, the sound begins to change and I hear that ghostly voice once more. Again and again, I hear it crying, "Let me in, Let me in!" But when I run to the window, there is no one there, and the only sound I can hear is the wind wuthering over the moors.

Wuthering Heights — that it is the name of the house where my story begins. I've often wished that I had never set foot inside its door…

13

I have just returned from Wuthering Heights – the loneliest house you could ever imagine. The ancient stone farmhouse stands high up on the moors, blank-faced and grim, with a hedge of stunted trees bent almost double by the wind. Wuthering Heights is the home of Mr. Heathcliff, who also owns Thrushcross Grange, the house where I am staying. So, once I had settled into my rooms at the Grange, I thought it would be polite to visit my landlord, up at the Heights.

It was a hard ride across the moors, and as I approached Wuthering Heights, I was pleased to see a man who I thought must be Heathcliff, leaning on his garden gate, and gazing out over the moors. He was tall and wild-looking, with a mane of thick, dark hair, and as I came nearer, he seemed to shrink away from me, scowling up from under heavy, black eyebrows.

"Mr. Heathcliff?" I asked politely.

The man nodded.

"Let my introduce myself, sir," I continued. "I am Mr. Lockwood, your new tenant, and I hope I won't be troubling you too much if…"

"I don't allow anyone to trouble me," he interrupted rudely. Then, after a pause, he added gruffly, "Walk in!"

Heathcliff showed me into a large sitting room. The room was dark and plainly furnished, with an enormous fireplace and some vicious-looking pistols hanging on the wall. In one corner, a huge hound

was curled up in a basket, surrounded by a mass of squealing puppies, and I could just make out some other large dogs hiding in the shadows.

I sat down by the fireside and tried to stroke one of the wolfish-looking beasts,

"You'd better leave her alone," growled Heathcliff, "she's not used to being spoiled."

Then he strode off in search of a servant, leaving me alone in the room.

Almost as soon as their master had disappeared, the beasts began to close in on me. Two shaggy-haired sheepdogs advanced menacingly towards me and others appeared from all corners of the room. I stayed very still in my chair, but couldn't resist pulling faces and winking at the dogs. This foolish action drove them into a frenzy, and soon they were attacking me from all sides, tugging at my clothes, and baring their teeth in a storm of snarling and yelping.

Fortunately for me, the housemaid arrived just in time. She swirled around the room swinging at the dogs with her heavy frying pan, and was just chasing away the last of them when her master returned.

"What the devil is the matter?" he asked angrily.

But I was angry too. "What the devil indeed!" I replied. "You might just as well leave your guests alone with a pack of tigers!"

At this, Heathcliff's face relaxed into a smile.

"Come, come," he said, "don't be flustered, Mr. Lockwood. Guests are so exceedingly rare in this house that I and my dogs hardly know how to look after them. Here, take a little wine with me. To your good health, sir!"

I decided to put the unfortunate incident behind me and gracefully accepted Heathcliff's offer of wine. Then we settled down by the fireplace and talked for almost an hour, discussing the moors and the history of the area. To my surprise, my landlord turned out to be a well-educated man, and I asked myself why a gentleman like him would choose to spend his life cut off from the rest of the world.

All the way back across the moors, I thought about Heathcliff and his lonely life, and by the time I reached the Grange, I had made up my mind. I would make a friend of him, whether he liked it or not.

The next day was cold and misty, but I was determined to see my new friend again, so as soon as lunch was over, I set off to walk the four miles to the Heights. But even before I reached the house, I was regretting my plan. I was shivering and exhausted, and the first flakes of snow were just starting to fall.

I hammered on the door until my knuckles tingled and the dogs howled.

"Wretched people," I shouted, shaking the door latch, "I'm freezing to death out here. Why don't you let me in?"

A vinegary-faced old servant stuck his head out of the window.

"The master's not at home. You'll have to go and find him out in the fields."

"Well, isn't there anyone here to let me in?"

"There's only the missus," the old man replied, "and she wouldn't open the door if you made that noise all night."

By this time, the snow had begun to fall heavily and I had just seized the knocker to start hammering again when a young man with a pitchfork appeared in the yard. He called to me to follow him and we soon arrived in the room where I had been before.

I cheered up greatly when I saw a large fire burning in the grate, and I was delighted to see the "missus", sitting next to a table laid for supper. I bowed and waited, thinking that she would offer me a seat, but she stayed completely silent, staring up at me from her chair. She was about eighteen years old and very slim, with fair, curling hair. She also had the most exquisite face I had ever seen, with small features and eyes which would have been irresistible, if only they had a less disagreeable expression.

"Rough weather!" I remarked to the beautiful young lady.

She stared at me without smiling.

"Sit down," said the young man, gruffly. "He'll be in soon."

I obeyed, and began to fondle the wretched dog that had caused me so much trouble on my last visit.

"A beautiful animal!" I started again. "Do you plan to keep her puppies, madam?"

"They're not mine," my charming hostess replied in a voice even more chilling than Heathcliff would have used.

"Ah, so these are your pets then?" I said, turning to a cushion full of something like cats.

"A strange choice of pets," she observed scornfully.

Unfortunately, the pets turned out to be a heap of dead rabbits! I cleared my throat again and tried repeating my comments on the weather.

"Well you shouldn't have come out," was all the rude young woman could say as she reached up for a canister of tea.

"Were you asked for tea?" she demanded.

"I would very much like a cup."

"But were you asked?"

"No," I said, half smiling. "But surely it's up to you, madam, to ask me that."

This reply seemed to make her even angrier, and she flung the teaspoon back into the canister and slumped into her chair, her lower lip pushed out, ready to cry.

All this time, the young man was standing in front of the fire, glaring at me as if I were his deadly enemy. I had thought at first that he must be a servant, but now I began to wonder – he seemed so proud, and made no effort at all to look after the lady of the house. I decided it would be best to ignore him, and after five minutes of awkward silence I was greatly relieved when Heathcliff arrived.

"You see sir, I have come to visit you again," I announced cheerfully, "but I'll need to stay for another half an hour until the snow has died down again."

"Half an hour?" said Heathcliff, shaking the snowflakes from his clothes. "I can tell you there's no chance of this snow stopping now. Whatever made you come out in weather like this?"

"Well perhaps one of your servants could guide me back across the moors? Could you spare me one for the night?"

"No, I could not."

Then Heathcliff turned to the young lady, "Are you going to make the tea?" he demanded.

"Is he having any?" she asked in disgust.

"Just get it ready," was all he said, in a voice so savage I drew back in shock. Was this the man I wanted to have as my friend?

As soon as the tea was ready, the four of us sat down to eat. I decided it was up to me to put everyone in a better mood.

"It's strange," I began, "how different people are. Some folks would feel very lonely up here, cut off from the rest of the world. But I'm sure, Mr. Heathcliff, you are perfectly happy, with your charming lady by your side…"

"My charming lady!" he interrupted, with a sneer on his face. "Where is she – my charming lady?"

"Mrs. Heathcliff, your wife, I mean."

"Oh – my wife! So you reckon she's become an angel and hovers around us here, even though she's dead and buried? Is that what you mean, sir?"

I realized I had made a terrible mistake. But then a new thought struck me – the rough young man who was sitting beside me must be Heathcliff's son and the lady's husband.

"Mrs. Heathcliff is my daughter-in-law," said

Heathcliff, confirming my guess.

"Ah, now I see," I said, turning to the lad who was busy slurping his tea, "so you, sir, are the fortunate husband of this good fairy."

But this was worse than before. The young man turned crimson and clenched his fist, as though he wanted to punch me in the face.

"Wrong again, sir," said Heathcliff. "We neither of us have the privilege of owning this 'good fairy' as you call her. Her husband is dead. I said she was my daughter-in-law, so she must have married my son."

"And this young man is –"

"Certainly not my son!"

"My name is Hareton Earnshaw," he growled angrily, "and you'd better make sure you respect it."

After that, no one said another word and we finished our meal in dismal silence.

The moment supper was over, I went straight to the window to check the weather. While we had been eating, the storm had grown much worse and now the sky was almost black. Thick snowflakes were whirling outside the window and I couldn't even see as far as the gate. There was no way I could find my way back to the Grange that night. I would have to spend the night at Wuthering Heights.

No one in that wretched house tried to make me welcome or even offered to find me a place to sleep, but eventually the housemaid, Zillah, took pity on me. She found me a candle and some blankets and led me upstairs, showing me into a small, cold room, that was almost completely empty of furniture.

I was just about to thank her, when she whispered to me, "Make as little noise as possible, sir. The master doesn't like anyone staying in this room."

Too tired to be curious about this warning, I slumped down on a window-seat and stared out at the snow. The ledge where I had placed my candle had a few tattered books piled up in one corner and seemed to be covered with writing scratched into the paint. At first, I took no notice of the scratches, but then I realized that they spelled out a name, repeated many times in all kinds of letters, large and small – *Catherine Earnshaw*, again and again, and then *Catherine Linton*, and sometimes *Catherine Heathcliff*. I puzzled over the names until my eyes began to close, but five minutes later I was jolted awake by the smell of burning leather – one of the books had fallen on top of the candle flame.

Drowsily, I opened the book and saw a name written in the front – *Catherine Earnshaw*, and underneath a date from over twenty years before. I soon discovered that all the books belonged to the same girl. They were a collection of schoolbooks, histories and sermons, most of them very dull. I was just dropping off to sleep again when I noticed a note scribbled in a margin...

"I wish my father was still alive. Hindley is so cruel to us. He makes H work in the fields all day and never allows us to play together. H and I are going to rebel. We will take our first steps tomorrow..."

But then the writing ended and I dozed off again,

dreaming of a swarm of Catherines – Catherine Earnshaw, Catherine Linton, Catherine Heathcliff – all jumbled up together, until my head was spinning.

Finally, I managed to drag myself into bed. But just as I was drifting off to sleep I became aware of a loud, insistent noise. Somewhere outside, a branch was knocking against the window, scratching and thumping in time to the wailing of the wind.

Eventually, I could bear it no longer. I climbed out of bed, determined to break off the branch and put an end to the noise. But when I tried to open the window, I found that it had been sealed tightly shut. By this time, I was so desperate to stop the knocking that I pushed my knuckles right through the glass. Then I stretched out my hand, ready to grasp the branch… but instead my fingers closed on a small, ice-cold hand!

I tried to pull back, but the icy fingers tightened their grip, and I heard a melancholy voice moaning,

"Let me in – let me in!"

"Who are you?" I shouted, struggling to be free.

"Catherine Linton," the shivery voice replied. "I've come home. I lost my way on the moor, but now I've come home."

I peered out into the snow and saw, very faintly, the outline of a young girl's face, staring back at me!

Terror made me cruel, and finding it impossible to shake off the creature's hand, I rubbed the delicate wrist across the broken glass, until the ledge was covered in blood. But still the hand kept its grip, driving me mad with fear, while the voice continued to wail, "Let me in!"

"How can I let you in," I said grimly, "if you hold my hand so tightly? You'll have to let me go if you want to come in."

As soon as the fingers relaxed, I snatched back my hand and blocked up

the hole with a pile of books. Then I covered my ears to keep out the sound of the terrible wailing.

I kept my ears covered for more than quarter of an hour, but the moment I listened again, I heard the mournful cry once more.

"Go away!" I shouted, "I'll never let you in – not if you beg for twenty years!"

"But it is twenty years," moaned the voice. "I've been wandering the moors for twenty years!"

Then the scratching began again and the books on the ledge started to shake. I tried to jump up, but found I couldn't move, so I opened my mouth and yelled as loudly as I could.

Almost immediately, the door was wrenched open and Heathcliff burst into the room. His face was as white as the walls around him and he was trembling from head to foot.

"Is anybody there?" he said in a half-whisper.

"It's only your guest," I announced, pulling myself together, "I was having a bad dream."

"God damn you, sir!" he replied, shaking so hard that he had to put down his candle. "Who showed you into this room? I've a good mind to turn them out into the snow this minute!"

"It was your housemaid, Zillah," I replied, dressing myself quickly, "and you can turn her out if you like, sir. I'm sure she deserves it, for letting me sleep in a room that's swarming with ghosts and goblins!"

"What do you mean?" roared Heathcliff. "And what do you think you're doing here? Lie down and finish the night, but for heaven's sake don't make that noise again. It sounded as though you were having your throat cut!"

"If the little fiend had got in, she probably would have strangled me to death!" I replied crossly. "I won't put up with your horrible ghosts a moment longer. And as for that vixen, Catherine Linton, or Earnshaw, or whatever she's called — she must have been a wicked little fiend. She told me she'd been walking the earth for twenty years — I expect she was being punished for her sins!"

"How dare you talk like that under my roof!" thundered Heathcliff.

"Don't worry, sir," I replied, pulling on the rest of my clothes as fast as I could. "I don't intend to spend another moment in this house!"

Heathcliff took no more notice of me. In seconds, he was at the window, forcing it wide open with incredible strength.

"Come in! Come in!" he sobbed, leaning out into the snow. "Oh, my heart's darling, hear me this time. Cathy, my darling, come in at last!"

But the ghost behaved as ghosts usually do, and showed no sign of ever having being there at all. Now there was nothing outside the window except the snow and wind, whirling around wildly in the dark. And, as I watched, the snowflakes blew into the room, and danced around madly, filling it with icy cold and blowing out the candle.

Heathcliff arrives

I spent the rest of the night trying to get some sleep on a hard kitchen bench, but as soon as it was light, I seized the chance to escape from Wuthering Heights. The moors were covered in billows of snow, and I lost count of the number of times I blundered off the path, sinking up to my waist in snow. When I finally reached the Grange, the clock was chiming twelve and I was too numb even to think. Nelly Dean, the housekeeper, made a great fuss of me, and I was soon sitting in my study, as feeble as a kitten, and almost too weak to enjoy the cheerful fire.

I stayed by the fire all afternoon, too exhausted to work, going over my strange adventures at Wuthering Heights. Every time I closed my eyes I saw the faces of the people I had met... mysterious, brooding Heathcliff, young, sulky Catherine and clumsy, silent Hareton. Why did they hate each other so much, and why were they all living up at the Heights together? But most of all I wondered about the wild, dark-haired girl at the window. Was she a ghost or a fiend? And what was she doing wandering over the moors?

Eventually, I decided to give up all thoughts of studying for the day, and when Nelly arrived with my supper, I asked her to sit with me for a while, hoping she would tell me more about the Heights.

"I understand you've lived at the Grange for a long time," I began. "Did you say it was eighteen years?"

"Yes, sir – I came to look after my mistress when she married."

"And who was your mistress, Nelly?" I asked.

"Her name was Catherine Earnshaw."

("Catherine Earnshaw!" I thought to myself. "Could this be the ghostly girl I'd seen at the window?")

"And what happened to Catherine Earnshaw?"

"She died, sir, soon after her marriage to Mr. Linton, but she had a daughter and I stayed on to look after her until she married and went to live at the Heights."

"So is that the young lady I saw last night?"

"Yes, sir, she's my young Miss Catherine, who I cared for all her life. But tell me, how is the poor girl now?"

"Mrs. Heathcliff? Well, I thought she looked healthy enough, and very beautiful, but she didn't seem happy."

Nelly sighed, "And what do you think of Heathcliff, Mr. Lockwood?"

"A rather rough fellow, I thought. Don't you agree?"

"Oh, he's as rough as a saw-edge and as hard as the rocks on the moor! But he's rich too."

"Whatever can have happened to make him like he is?"

"Well that's a long story, sir. His life is like a cuckoo's... I know all about it, except where he was born and who his parents were, and how he grew so rich that he pushed all the other birds out of the nest."

I was sure I wouldn't sleep that night until I knew more. My head felt hot, but the rest of my body was icy cold, and I felt strangely excited by everything that had happened up at the Heights. I asked Nelly to stay with me and tell me more, so she settled herself comfortably and started her story…

Before I came to live at the Grange, she began, I lived at Wuthering Heights. My mother was housekeeper to old Mr. Earnshaw and his wife, and I ran errands for the family and hung around the farm, doing any jobs they wanted me to do. We were so much part of the family, that I was even allowed to play with the children – young Master Hindley and Miss Cathy.

One summer morning, we were all playing together when Mr. Earnshaw came downstairs, ready for a journey,

"I'm going to Liverpool today. So what shall I bring you? You can chose anything you like, but it must be small because I'm walking there and back – sixty miles each way – and that's a long hike!"

Hindley asked for a violin, and Cathy, who was only six years old but could ride any horse in the stable, chose a riding whip. The master didn't forget me either, and promised to bring me a pocketful of apples. Then he kissed his children goodbye and set off across the moors.

The three days that Mr. Earnshaw was away seemed a terribly long time – and little Cathy asked again and again when her father would be home. We expected him back at tea time, but in the end it was just after eleven when the sitting room door opened and he burst into the room. He threw himself into a chair, laughing and groaning, and told us all to leave him alone because he was half dead.

"And on top of all the walking, I've been nearly punched to death!" he said, opening up his overcoat, which he held bundled up in his arms.

"Take a look at this," he said to his wife, "I've never been so beaten by anything in my life!"

We all crowded around, and saw a dirty, ragged, black-haired boy! He was big enough to walk and talk, but he only stared around and muttered some nonsense at us that no one could understand. I was frightened, and Mrs. Earnshaw wanted to fling the creature straight out of doors.

"Are you insane?" she asked her husband angrily. "What made you bring this gypsy brat into our house, when we have children of our own to feed and care for?"

The master tried to explain what had happened, but he was half dead from exhaustion. All I could understand, in between his wife's scolding and shouting, was that he had found the child starving and homeless in the streets of Liverpool, where he had picked it up and asked around for its owner. No one knew who the boy belonged to, and he was much too kindhearted to leave the child alone to its fate, so he decided to bring it home with him.

Eventually, my mistress grumbled herself calm and

Mr. Earnshaw told me I must wash the creature and give it clean clothes to wear. Hindley and Cathy had been silent up until then, but now they both began searching in their father's pockets for the presents he'd promised them. When Hindley pulled out what was left of his violin, he burst into tears like a baby, even though he was fourteen years old. And when Cathy learned that her whip had been lost, she took her revenge by making faces at the creature, until her father told her to stop. Both the

children refused to have the boy in their room, so when I had washed and dressed him I put him out on the landing, hoping he might be gone by the morning. But somehow he managed to creep into the master's room and the next morning I was punished for my cruelty.

So this was how the cuckoo came to live in the Earnshaws' nest. Mr. Earnshaw called him Heathcliff – the only name he ever had – and he and Miss Cathy soon became great friends. But Hindley hated him, and when I saw how the master made such a fuss of him I began to hate him too. Hindley and I teased and tormented Heathcliff whenever we could, and Mrs. Earnshaw never spoke up for him, even when she knew that we were in the wrong.

Heathcliff was a silent, patient child, perhaps hardened to bad treatment by everything he'd suffered already in his life. He put up with Hindley's punches without complaining, and my pinches simply made him draw in his breath in silence. When Mr. Earnshaw discovered what was happening to Heathcliff, he was furious, and he soon became much more fond of him than he was of his own children. So, from the very beginning, Heathcliff caused bad feelings in the family.

By the time Mrs. Earnshaw died, less than two years later, Master Hindley had learned to see his father as an enemy. He believed that Heathcliff had stolen his place in the family, and grew very bitter about the way his life had changed.

A few years after Mrs. Earnshaw died, my master became very ill. He spent most of his time in a chair by the fireplace, growing more and more irritable. He was especially angry with Hindley for treating Heathcliff so badly and in the end he decided to send his son away to college.

Once Hindley was out of the way, I thought at last we would have some peace, but Miss Cathy was much too wild to settle down quietly. She was always getting into mischief – singing and laughing and larking around, and teasing anyone who wouldn't join in her games. She drove us all to distraction, but she had the sweetest smile and so no one could stay angry with her for long.

One thing was certain – young Cathy was much too fond of Heathcliff. She hated being apart from him, and Heathcliff felt just the same about her. She loved giving orders, and Heathcliff would do anything she wanted. It made her father furious, to see how she ruled over the boy.

One evening, when Cathy was quieter than usual, she came and sat on the floor beside her father and leaned her head against his knee. Heathcliff lay with his head in Cathy's lap, while Mr. Earnshaw stroked her hair.

"Why can't you always be a good girl, Cathy?" he murmured.

"And why can't you always be a good man, father?" she laughed. Mr. Earnshaw looked sad to hear this response, and when Cathy saw that she had upset him, she gave her father a kiss and said she would sing him to sleep. She began to sing very quietly, until his head dropped down onto his chest and he fell into a sound sleep. I was glad to see the old man sleeping so well. But when it was time to go to bed, Cathy put her arms around his neck to say goodnight, and screamed out in fright, "Oh, he's dead, Heathcliff! He's dead!"

Then they both started crying pitifully, and I joined in too.

Later that evening, I heard Cathy and Heathcliff talking together. They were picturing their father happy in heaven, far away from his troubles on earth. I cried as I listened to them, because I was afraid of what might happen next. And I wished that we could all be saved from the troubles that lay ahead.

Heathcliff and Cathy

Hindley Earnshaw came back to Wuthering Heights for the funeral, and much to our surprise he brought a wife with him. Her name was Frances and she was very young and lively, with eyes that sparkled as brightly as diamonds. I did notice that climbing the stairs made her breathe very fast, and she had a troublesome cough, but I had no idea then what those signs could mean.

Hindley soon made sure that we knew who was master. He ordered Joseph and me to stay in the kitchen and leave the rest of the house to him and his wife. Cathy was allowed to continue her lessons, but Heathcliff had to work on the farm. He ate all his meals with the servants and slept in an attic room in the roof.

At first, Heathcliff put up with this treatment patiently, because he still saw Cathy every day. She taught him everything she learned and spent all her spare time playing with him. Hindley didn't care what Cathy and Heathcliff did together so long as they kept out of his way, and they soon became completely wild. Their greatest treat was to run off up to the moors, and stay out there by themselves all day. It frightened me to see the two of them growing up like untamed animals – I was afraid of how things might end.

One rainy Sunday evening, Cathy and Heathcliff were in trouble for making too much noise, so Hindley sent them out of the house. But when I called them in for supper they were nowhere to be seen. I spent the rest of the evening searching for them, but at nine o'clock Hindley bolted all the doors, and swore he wouldn't let them in that night. Everyone went to bed, but I was much too worried to sleep so I sat by my bedroom window listening for noises. Eventually, I heard footsteps coming up the lane and saw the light of a lantern glimmering through the gate. I threw a shawl over my head and ran out to find them.

I expected to see the two of them by the gate, but there was only Heathcliff, soaked to the skin.

"Where's Miss Cathy?" I called out in fright.

"At Thrushcross Grange," he replied, "and I should be there too, but they didn't have the manners to ask me to stay."

"Well, you'll be in trouble when the master hears about this," I said crossly. "But why did you go so far away?"

"Just let me get out of my wet clothes, Nelly, and I'll tell you all about it."

I warned Heathcliff to be quiet, to avoid waking Hindley, and while he undressed, he told me the whole story...

"Cathy and I were running over the moors

together, when we saw the lights on in the Grange, and decided to see how Edgar and Isabella Linton spent their evenings. Do you think they are forced to stand shivering outside like us, Nelly, while their parents roast themselves beside the fire? So, we raced all the way from the Heights to Thrushcross Park without stopping once, and Cathy lost her shoes. Then we crept through a broken hedge and groped our way up a path, and stood on a flowerpot just under a low window.

"The living room curtains were still open so we could see right inside, and it was just like a palace – all crimson and gold. Edgar and Isabella had the room to themselves, and can you guess what they were doing? Isabella was lying screaming on the floor, shrieking as if witches were pushing needles into her skin, and Edgar was standing by the fire, weeping like a baby! And what do you think all the fuss was about? In the middle of the table was a little dog, shaking its paw and yelping – and nearly pulled in two by the spoiled brats! We laughed out loud at the idiots! What sort of fun do you think that was to quarrel over a stupid puppy dog? And when would you catch me arguing with Cathy or taking anything she wanted?"

"Anyway, we laughed so much that Cathy fell off the flowerpot. The Lintons heard the noise and raced to the door, and then you should have heard them howl! 'Oh, mama, mama! Oh, papa! Oh, mama come here!' They really did cry out like that! We both made

horrible noises to frighten them some more, but then we decided we had better run away.

"We were running as fast as we could, when Cathy suddenly fell over.

" 'Run, Heathcliff, run!' she said. 'They've let their bulldog loose and he's got me by the ankle!'

"I could hear the dog's terrible snorting, but Cathy didn't yell out – she would have been ashamed to cry. I started swearing at the beast and had just managed to find a stone to thrust between its jaws, when at last a servant appeared with a lantern and hauled the beast away.

"The man lifted Cathy up in his arms. She had fainted – not from fear, I'm sure, but from pain – and I followed him into the house, shouting and swearing.

" 'What's happening, Robert?' called Mr. Linton from the entrance.

" 'Skulker's caught a little girl, sir,' he replied, 'and there's a lad here too, who looks like a real villain. They're probably a pair of robbers planning to creep through the window and murder us all in our beds.'

"Robert pulled me under the lamp so they could all take a look at me. Mrs. Linton put on her spectacles and peered in horror, and the cowardly children crept closer to her skirts.

" 'What a frightful thing!' snivelled Isabella. 'Lock him up in the cellar, papa. He's a wicked boy!'

"While they were examining me, Edgar was staring at Cathy.

" 'That's Miss Earnshaw!' he whispered to his mother. 'And look how her foot is bleeding and bruised!'

" 'Miss Earnshaw?' cried Mrs. Linton. 'Miss Earnshaw – roaming the countryside with a gypsy boy? But you're right, it is the girl – and she may be lame for life!'

40

" 'How can her brother allow her out so late?' said Mr. Linton. 'I've heard he neglects her terribly. And who's this she has with her? I believe it's the boy old Earnshaw found in Liverpool...'

" 'A wicked boy, in any case,' his wife interrupted, 'and quite unfit for a decent house. Send him away from here immediately!'

"Robert dragged me into the garden and locked the door behind me. But I crept back to the window, determined to shatter it into fragments if Cathy wanted to escape. The curtains were still open, and I could see everything. They had laid Cathy on a sofa and a servant was washing her feet, Isabella had emptied a plateful of cakes into her lap and Edgar was just standing there, gaping open-mouthed. After a while, they started to comb her beautiful hair, and gave her a pair of slippers to wear. Then they wheeled the sofa closer to the fire, and I left her, as cheerful as could be, surrounded by the Lintons, all gazing at her with their empty blue eyes... So you see, Nelly, the Lintons have my Cathy, and who knows when I shall see her again?"

In the end, Miss Cathy stayed at Thrushcross Grange for five weeks. By the end of that time, her ankle was completely better, and her manners had greatly improved as well. Mrs. Linton bought Cathy lots of fine new clothes, and when she returned to us, just before Christmas, she was a very different girl. Instead of the wild, hatless creature who used to rush into the house and squeeze the breath out of us all, a very dignified young lady arrived at the front door. She wore a beautiful silk dress and a long velvet cloak that she had to lift up when she walked. On her head was a velvet hat with a feather, and her wild hair had been tamed and arranged in ringlets around her face.

Hindley was delighted.

"Why Cathy, you're quite a beauty! I would hardly have recognized you – you look like a young lady now. Isabella Linton is nothing compared to her, is she, Frances?"

"Isabella does not have Cathy's looks," replied his wife coolly. "But we must make sure she doesn't grow wild again."

Cathy kissed me carefully, anxious not to disarrange her hair – and then she looked around the room for Heathcliff. He was hard to find at first, but at last she saw him, skulking behind a chair. I could see he was ashamed to be seen beside such a sparkling young lady – and he certainly did look a sight. His clothes were covered with grime and dust, his hair was tangled, and his face and hands were a dismal shade of grey.

"Come along Heathcliff, there's no need to hide," cried Hindley, obviously enjoying the boy's shame. "You can come and welcome Miss Catherine, just like the other servants."

Cathy raced towards her old friend and covered him with kisses just like she used to do, but then she stopped and drew back in surprise, laughing out loud, "I'd forgotten how black and cross you look, Heathcliff, and how funny and grim! But that's because I'm used to Edgar and Isabella, with their pretty golden hair."

Heathcliff stood silent and still as a stone.

"Well, Heathcliff, have you forgotten me?"

"Why don't you talk to Miss Cathy?" said Hindley condescendingly. "Just occasionally, that is allowed."

"I shall not!" shouted the boy, racing from the room, "And I won't stand being laughed at, I just won't bear it!"

Later that day, I went to find Heathcliff. He was in the stables, giving the horses their evening feed.

"Come into the kitchen with me, Heathcliff, and let me dress you neatly before Miss Cathy comes down. Then you can sit by the fire and have a long chat together."

But Heathcliff kept his head turned away from me.

"Are you coming, Heathcliff? There's some supper waiting for you, but I'll need a good half hour to clean you up first."

I waited for five minutes, but there was no answer, so I left him to sulk on his own. Cathy ate supper with her brother and sister-in-law, but Heathcliff marched straight up to bed without stopping to eat.

The next day, the Linton children were invited to the Heights for a Christmas party. We had prepared a great feast and there were presents for everyone… except Heathcliff. Mrs. Linton had accepted the Earnshaws' invitation on condition that her little darlings were kept well away from that 'naughty, swearing boy'.

Heathcliff got up very early that morning and went out walking on the moors, and when he came back, all the family was away at church. He hung around the kitchen in awkward silence for a while and then he finally spoke.

"Nelly, make me decent. I'm going to be good."

"And about time too, Heathcliff," I replied. "You've really upset Miss Cathy. I bet she's sorry she ever came home! She must think you envy her because the Lintons are her friends."

"Did she say she was upset?" he asked, looking serious.

"She cried when I told her you were off on the moors this morning."

"Well, I cried last night," he replied, "and I had more reason to be sad."

"Perhaps you deserve it, for being so proud and stubborn. But I'll see what I can do to make you look good. And by the time I've finished with you, you'll be so handsome that Edgar Linton will seem like a doll beside you."

I made Heathcliff wash his grimy face and combed his great mane of hair. And when he was dressed in his clean clothes, he looked as handsome as a prince.

"Now, if only you'd try smiling, instead of scowling like thunder, you'd be worth ten of young Edgar. Although you're younger than him, you're taller and broader, and you don't go crying for your mama all the time!"

So I chattered on, and Heathcliff gradually lost his frown and began to look quite pleasant. Then, all at once, we heard the rumble of wheels outside. Heathcliff ran to the window, just in time to see the Lintons climbing down from their carriage, smothered in cloaks and furs. Cathy raced out to meet her two young friends and brought them into the house. Then she settled them down by the fire, which quickly put some warmth into their pale, doll-like faces.

I urged Heathcliff to hurry down and show them how he had changed, and he willingly obeyed. But, as luck would have it, he met Hindley in the corridor. The master was far from pleased to see Heathcliff looking so clean and cheerful, and he called out quickly to Joseph, "Keep this fellow out of the room – and lock him in the attic until dinner is over. He'll be cramming his fingers into the pies, and stealing the fruit, if he's left alone for a minute."

"No sir," I couldn't stop myself from answering, "he won't touch anything – and I think he should have his share of the treats as well."

"He'll have a share of my hand, if I catch him downstairs again," roared Hindley, reaching out to grab Heathcliff by the hair. "Just wait till I get hold of these elegant locks – let's see if I can pull them a little bit longer!"

"They're long enough already," observed Master Linton, peeping round the door. "I'm surprised he doesn't have a headache, with that colt's mane over his eyes!"

I'm sure that Edgar meant no harm, but Heathcliff couldn't bear such impertinence from someone he already saw as his rival. So he seized a dish of apple sauce – the first thing he could find – and poured it all over Edgar's head! Edgar instantly burst into tears, and Cathy and Isabella came hurrying to help.

In an instant, Hindley had grabbed Heathcliff by the collar and marched him up to his room, where he obviously thrashed him soundly, because he returned quite red in the face. I found a dishcloth and rubbed at Edgar's nose and mouth quite roughly, telling him it served him right for interfering. Then his sister began to cry and say she wanted to go home, but Cathy just stood there, staring in horror.

"You shouldn't have upset Heathcliff like that," she told the snivelling Edgar. "Now Hindley will beat him – and I hate it when he hurts Heathcliff. I can't eat my dinner now. Why did you speak to him, Edgar?"

"But I didn't," sobbed the boy, escaping from my hands. "I promised mama I wouldn't say a word to him, and I didn't!"

"Well there's no need to cry!" replied Cathy scornfully. "You're not dead. And you stop crying too, Isabella – has anyone hurt you?"

"Now children – time for dinner," said Hindley, bustling into the room. "Let's all enjoy the feast!"

Hindley served up large helpings of food, and his wife kept up a stream of cheerful talk. Gradually, the children recovered and everyone began to enjoy their meal… or at least everyone did except Cathy. I watched her lift a mouthful of food to her lips, and quickly put it down again. Then she dropped her fork and dived under the table to hide her tears. And all through the afternoon I saw that she was in agony, longing to get away and find Heathcliff again.

In the evening, there was dancing in the hall and the house was filled with cheerful music, but I noticed that Miss Cathy was desperate to escape. As soon as she could get away from her guests, she set off up the stairs, saying that the music sounded better from up there. I followed her up to the attic room where Heathcliff was kept prisoner, and left the poor things alone, talking to each other through his locked door.

Later that evening, I persuaded Miss Cathy to come downstairs and say goodbye to her guests. Then I took Heathcliff to the kitchen to give him some food. He hadn't eaten a thing since lunchtime the day before, but he soon pushed the food away, and sat at the table in silence with his head in his hands. At last, I asked him what he was thinking and he replied very solemnly, "I'm trying to work out how I shall pay Hindley back. And I don't care how long I wait, just so long as I do it at last."

Edgar and Cathy

The next summer, Hindley's son, Hareton, was born. I was working in the fields when a girl came running up from the house, calling to me as she ran,

"Oh such a beautiful boy!" she panted. "The finest lad that ever breathed. But Doctor Kenneth says the mistress won't last. He says she's been sick for months. I heard him tell Mr. Hindley that now she's had the baby, she won't keep on fighting any more, and he reckons she'll be dead before the winter. You must come home straightaway, Nelly, to look after the baby. You're going to be his nurse, and care for him day and night, and soon he'll be all yours when the mistress is dead!"

"But is she so very ill?" I asked, flinging down my rake.

"I guess she is, although she tries to look cheerful," replied the girl, "and she talks as though she'll see her son grow up to be a man. She's out of her mind with joy because he's such a beauty!"

I hurried home as fast as I could, excited to see the child, although I was sad for Hindley too. He loved only two people in the world – his wife and himself – and I didn't know how he would live without her.

When I reached Wuthering Heights, Hindley was at the front door, and I asked him how the baby was.

"Nearly ready to run around!" he replied, putting on a cheerful smile.

"And the Mistress?" I dared to ask. "The doctor says she's…"

"Damn the doctor!" he interrupted. "Frances is quite well – she'll be perfectly fine by this time next week. But will you please tell her not to talk, so she can recover fast… Doctor Kenneth has left orders that she must be quiet."

I gave this message to his wife, who replied cheerfully, "I hardly say a word, Nelly, but each time I do, he leaves the room crying. Well, I promise I won't talk again, but that doesn't mean that I can't laugh at him."

Poor soul! Until a week before her death, young Mrs. Earnshaw was so cheerful and brave, and Hindley insisted furiously that her health was improving every day. When Doctor Kenneth warned him that his wife had reached the stage of her illness when his medicines were useless, Hindley replied stubbornly, "I know she doesn't need them. She's perfectly well now. She's had a fever, but that's all gone."

Hindley told his wife the same story, and she seemed to believe him. But one night, while she was leaning on his shoulder and saying that she thought she would get up tomorrow, she was seized with a coughing fit – just a very small one. Hindley held her in his arms and she put her arms around his neck. Then her face changed and she was dead.

As the serving girl had predicted, I was completely in charge of young Hareton after Mrs. Earnshaw died. Hindley left everything to me, only insisting that he should never have to hear his baby cry. He was desperate with grief for his wife, and spent his days drinking and cursing, blaming God and everyone around him for sending him such a punishment. The servants couldn't bear this treatment long, and one by one they left the Heights. Very soon, only Joseph and I were left to take care of the house.

Hindley's bad temper and drunkenness set a terrible example for the children, and his treatment of Heathcliff was enough to turn a saint into a fiend. But the boy put up with it all without complaining, and even seemed to delight in seeing Hindley sink lower and lower. Eventually, everyone stopped calling at the Heights. Miss Cathy's tutor had long since gone, and the only visitors we had were young Isabella and Edgar Linton. Of course, Edgar was terrified of Hindley, but he would have braved anything for a chance to see Cathy.

By the time Miss Cathy was fifteen years old, she was the most beautiful girl for miles around. But she could be wild and headstrong when she didn't get her way. Heathcliff was equally stubborn, and he had become very rough. For a while he struggled to keep up his studying, but by the time he was sixteen he had given up reading and writing completely. His clothes were always filthy and he had a permanent scowl on his face. When he wasn't working, Cathy and he were still constant companions, but he had stopped showing any affection for her, and he shrank away with angry suspicion from her hugs and kisses.

One afternoon, I was helping Miss Cathy into her best silk dress, when Heathcliff arrived at the door. Hindley was away and it was raining hard, so Heathcliff had made up his mind to spend the rest of the day with his friend. But when he saw Cathy's fine dress, his face fell.

"Cathy, are you going out this afternoon?" he asked gruffly.

"No, it's raining," was her scornful reply.

"Then why are you wearing that silk dress? Nobody's coming here, I hope."

"Not that I know of," stammered Cathy. "But you should be in the fields now, Heathcliff. It's an hour past dinner time."

"I'm not doing any more work today. I'm going to stay with you."

Cathy frowned and thought for a few minutes. Then she began, "Isabella and Edgar Linton talked about calling this afternoon. As it's raining they probably won't come, but if they do, you'll have to put up with their rudeness to you."

"Tell Nelly to say you're busy," Heathcliff said roughly. "Don't turn me away for those pitiful friends of yours. Tell them to go, so you can be with me."

This made Cathy very angry. "And why should I always be with you?" she demanded. "What do you ever talk about? You might as well be a baby for anything you say to amuse me!"

Heathcliff turned white. "You never told me before that I talked too little, or that you hated my company, Cathy!"

"It's no company at all, when people know nothing and say nothing," she muttered.

Heathcliff stood up suddenly, but before he could reply, they heard the sound of a horse's hooves outside, and Edgar was at the door.

It was hard not to notice the difference between the two young men as one of them came into the room and the other went out. To me, it seemed like exchanging a wild, windswept moor for a beautiful, sunlit valley. And their way of talking was just as different as their looks. Edgar had a soft, gentle-sounding voice, while Heathcliff's voice was gruff and harsh.

I lingered over my dusting.

"What are you doing there, Nelly?" Cathy snapped.

"My work, miss," I replied.

Hindley had ordered me not to leave his sister alone with Edgar, but Cathy had other ideas. She stepped behind me and whispered crossly, "Go away, Nelly, we want to be alone!"

"But this is a good chance to get on with my work, while Mr. Hindley is away."

Cathy was annoyed. Assuming that Edgar couldn't see her, she pinched me spitefully on the arm.

"Oh, Miss Cathy!" I yelled out in pain. "That was a mean trick! You've no right to hurt me like that."

"I didn't touch you, you lying creature," she cried, her fingers tingling to pinch me again.

But I was determined to show Edgar what she was like, so I held out my arm where a bruise was already forming, "What's this then?" I replied.

Cathy stamped her foot, hesitated for a moment, and then slapped me hard on the cheek, making my eyes fill with water.

"Catherine, love, Catherine!" Edgar said gently, shocked to see how violent she could be.

But Cathy took no notice. "Please leave the room now, Nelly!" she repeated, trembling all over.

At this point, little Hareton burst into tears, sobbing his complaints about "Wicked Aunt Cathy" and, before he could escape, Cathy had turned on him, and was shaking the poor child until he turned purple. Edgar stepped forward to rescue the boy, and the next minute he was amazed to feel the force of Cathy's hand on the side of his head.

As soon as he had recovered, Edgar headed straight for the door. His face was very pale and his mouth was quivering noticeably.

"That's right," I thought to myself. "Let this be a warning to you to get out fast. It's good for you to see what she's really like."

"Where are you going?" demanded Cathy, quickly

moving in front of the door.

Edgar swerved and tried to pass.

"You mustn't go!" she cried energetically.

"I must and I shall!"

"No," she insisted, holding onto the door handle, "not yet, Edgar Linton. You mustn't leave me in such a temper, or I shall be miserable all night, and I refuse to be made miserable by you."

"Do you think I can stay here, after what you've done to me?" he replied. "You've made me afraid and ashamed of you, Catherine. I won't be back again."

At this, Cathy's eyes began to fill with tears.

"And you told a deliberate lie!" Edgar continued.

"I did not," she cried passionately. "I did nothing deliberately. Well, go, if that's what you want – leave me now. And as for me, I'll cry – I'll cry myself sick."

And she dropped down onto her knees and began to sob as though her heart would break.

Edgar reached as far as the courtyard before he hesitated. I decided I would try to send him away.

"Miss Cathy is dreadfully stubborn, sir!" I called

out. "You'd better go straight home, or she'll make herself sick just to spite us."

The soft thing turned back and looked through the window.

"Ah," I thought, "there's no saving him now – he's doomed, and he's going to fly straight to his fate!"

And so he did. A minute later, Edgar had turned and hurried back into the house. When I knocked on the door half an hour later, to tell Cathy and Edgar that Hindley had come home raging drunk, I saw that their quarrel had brought them closer together. It had broken down the barriers of shyness between them and allowed them to tell each other that they were in love.

The news of Hindley's return sent Edgar rushing to his horse and Cathy to her room. I ran to take the bullets out of Hindley's gun and to hide little Hareton – when my master returned from a day's drinking none of us was safe. Hindley strode into the kitchen, just in time to see me stuffing his son into a closet. Poor Hareton was so terrified of his father's rages that he would stay quiet and still wherever I put him.

"There, I've caught you at it, Nelly," Hindley shouted. "Don't you dare keep my own son away from me or I'll force you to swallow the carving knife. And don't think I wouldn't do it, because I've just crammed Doctor Kenneth headfirst into Blackhorse marsh."

Hindley seized the child roughly. "Are you trying

to hide from me, Hareton?" he snarled. "And why do you scream at me as if I were a goblin?"

Hareton shrank back in terror, but Hindley snatched him up in his arms.

"What's the matter with the brat?" he roared. "Why won't you talk to your father? By heavens, I've reared a monster!"

Hareton struggled to get away, screaming and kicking as his father climbed the stairs. I panted after them, crying out that he would kill the child, and I was just at the top of the stairs, when he swung the boy over the banisters.

I was about to reach out and rescue Hareton, when Hindley leaned forward to listen to a noise, forgetting for a moment what he held in his hands.

"Who's that?" he called, as someone entered the hall below.

Heathcliff had just got in. At that very moment, Hareton struggled to be free, and fell.

We had hardly had time to react before we realized the child was safe. Heathcliff arrived just in time, and he caught the boy in his arms. Then he set Hareton on his feet and looked up to see what had happened.

As soon as Heathcliff saw Hindley leaning over the banisters, he realized what he had done – and his face turned black. He was clearly in agony at the thought that he had lost the chance to take his revenge on Hindley. I raced to comfort little Hareton, pressing him against my heart, while Hindley walked down the stairs more slowly, suddenly sober and shaken.

"It's your fault Nelly," Hindley said, roughly. "You should have kept him out of my way. Is he injured at all?"

"Injured!" I cried, angrily. "It's a miracle he's not dead. I wonder his mother doesn't rise from her grave to see how you treat him."

Hindley reached out to his son, who started screaming again.

"Don't you dare touch him!" I shouted. "He hates you – we all hate you. What a happy family you've created here."

"And it's going to get worse than this," he laughed grimly. "So get out of my sight, all of you, before I hurt you some more." And with that he seized a bottle of brandy and poured himself a drink.

"It's a pity he can't kill himself with drink," muttered Heathcliff as he left the hall.

I went into the kitchen and sat down by the fire to comfort my little lamb. Heathcliff was nowhere to be seen, so I imagined he was working outside.

I was rocking Hareton on my knee, when Miss Cathy appeared at the door.

"Are you alone, Nelly?" she asked softly.

"Yes," I said briefly, not yet ready to forgive her for her spitefulness earlier that day.

"And where is Heathcliff?"

"At work in the stables, I believe."

There was a long pause while I watched some drops of water fall from her cheeks onto the stone floor. Then she knelt down beside me.

"Nelly, will you keep a secret?" she asked, with a look that made all my temper melt away.

"Is it worth keeping?" I replied, less sulkily.

"Yes, and it worries me so much I must let it out. I want to know what I should do... Today, Edgar Linton asked me to marry him, and I've given him an answer. But before I say what it was – please tell me what you think my answer should have been."

"Really, Miss Cathy. How can I know? But after the scene this afternoon, I think you should refuse him. If Edgar asked you to marry him after that, he must be either stupid or insane."

"If you talk to me like that, I won't tell you any more," she answered peevishly. "I've accepted him, Nelly. Now tell me quickly, was I wrong?"

"Well, if you've accepted him, what's the good of asking me what to do? You've given him your word and you can't take it back."

"But tell me if I should have done it – please!" she cried out.

"Well," I said slowly. "The most important question is, do you love Mr. Edgar?"

"Anyone would love him, of course I do."

"But why do you love him, Miss Cathy?"

"Well, because he is handsome and pleasant to be with."

"Bad reasons," was my reply.

"And because he's young and cheerful."

"Bad again."

"And because he will be rich and I will be the richest woman for miles around, and I will be proud to have such a husband."

"Worst of all! You realize that he won't always be handsome and young, and he may not always be rich either."

"Well he is now, and I can only think of the present."

"Well then – that settles it. If you're only thinking of the present, then you should marry Mr. Linton."

"I don't want your permission, Nelly. I simply want to know whether you think I am right."

"Well," I continued, "what's the problem? If you love Edgar and he loves you, everything seems easy. Tell me where's the obstacle there?"

"In my heart!" cried Cathy passionately. "Because, in my heart, I'm convinced that I'm wrong."

"Well that's very strange. I don't understand you at all."

"But that's my secret, Nelly! Don't you see? And, if you don't make fun of me, I'll try to explain how I feel…"

Cathy's face grew sadder and her hands began to tremble.

"Nelly," she said suddenly, after a few minutes' silence. "Do you ever dream strange dreams?"

"Well, yes, I do – now and then."

"So do I," she answered. "I dreamed once I was in heaven, but heaven didn't seem to be my home and I broke my heart crying to come back to earth again. And the angels were so angry with me that they flung me out on the middle of the moors, and then I woke up, sobbing for joy. And that is why, Nelly, I cannot marry Edgar!

"I've no more right to marry Edgar than I have to be in heaven. And if my wicked brother hadn't brought Heathcliff so low, I would never have thought of it. But Heathcliff is so much beneath me now that it would degrade me to marry him, so he will never know how much I love him. And I don't love him because he's handsome, Nelly, but because he's more myself than I am. Whatever our souls are made of, his and mine

61

are the same, and Edgar's is as different as a moonbeam from lightning!"

Before Cathy had finished talking, I realized that Heathcliff was creeping out of the room. He'd been lying behind the kitchen bench all the time and had heard almost everything we said. He stayed until he heard Cathy say that it would degrade her to marry him, and then he silently left the room.

I left Hareton sitting on the bench, and went to the stove to start preparing supper. But Cathy hadn't finished yet.

"Nelly, do you think Heathcliff ever thinks about love or marriage? Surely he doesn't know what being in love is?"

"I don't see why he shouldn't know as well as you," I replied. "And if he is in love with you, he's the most unfortunate creature ever born. Because as soon as you become Mrs. Linton, he'll lose his love and his only friend. Have you thought about how he'll cope – how he'll be completely alone in the world? Because, Miss Cathy..."

"Heathcliff alone?" Cathy interrupted. "But who is going to separate us? No one will do that, as long as I live. Every Linton on the face of the Earth could melt into nothing before I'd agree to give up Heathcliff. He'll be as important to me when I marry as he has always been, and Edgar must just learn to like him too. And of course Edgar will, when he understands how I feel.

"I can see you think I'm a heartless wretch, Nelly.

But if Heathcliff and I were married, we would be beggars. And if I marry Edgar, I can help Heathcliff to rise, and escape from the clutches of my brother."

"Do you really think you'll persuade Edgar to help Heathcliff?" I asked. "You won't find him as easy to bend as you think. This is your worst reason yet for marrying him."

"It's not," she replied, "it's the best. Everything I do is linked to Heathcliff because it's impossible for us to be separated. My love for Linton is like the leaves on the trees but my love for Heathcliff is like the rocks on the moors. He is always in my mind – so don't ever talk of separation again…"

She stopped, and buried her face in my dress, but I jerked it away.

"I can't make any sense of your talk, miss," I said. "It seems to me you don't understand what it means to be married, or else you're a very wicked girl."

That night, there was one of the worst thunderstorms I have ever known. We even feared that the house might be struck down. Heathcliff stayed out all night, and Cathy spent most of the night in the storm, searching desperately for her friend. By morning, she was exhausted, but Heathcliff was nowhere to be seen. He didn't return that day, or any day after that. It was to be a very long time before we saw him again.

After Heathcliff disappeared, Miss Cathy was very ill. For weeks she lay in a fever, tossing and turning on her bed. Doctor Kenneth visited many times and drained several pints of blood from her, but this only seemed to make her wilder. At times, we were afraid she might throw herself down the stairs or even out of the window! But eventually, the fever grew weaker, and she began to recover slowly.

Old Mrs. Linton came to visit Cathy many times, and as soon as she was strong enough to travel, the kind lady insisted that Cathy should be moved to Thrushcross Grange. To tell the truth, I was relieved to be rid of Cathy for a while – she was a difficult patient and I had young Hareton to care for as well. But poor Mrs. Linton had reason to regret her kindness, because both she and her husband caught the fever from Cathy and died within a few days of each other.

After several months at the Grange, our young lady returned to the Heights, prouder and more passionate than ever. One day, when she provoked me beyond endurance, I dared to blame her for Heathcliff's disappearance. And after that, she refused to speak to me for months, apart from giving me orders and commands.

The months that followed Miss Cathy's illness were hard for us all. The doctor told us that she should be given her own way whenever possible, in case one of her terrible rages led to a deadly fit. And Cathy certainly made the most of his warning. She soon became so willful that she refused to be contradicted on anything. But while the rest of us fumed in silence, Edgar Linton was quite unable to see any faults in her. He was madly in love with Cathy, and on the day of their wedding at Gimmerton Church, he sincerely believed he was the happiest man on earth.

A surprising visitor

At this point in my housekeeper's story she glanced up at the clock, and was amazed to see that it was half past one. She wouldn't hear of staying a second longer, and I suddenly realized just how tired I was. I dragged my aching body off to bed, and spent a troubled night, dreaming of Wuthering Heights.

In the morning, I woke up with a throbbing head and a sore throat, which developed into a nasty case of flu. For the next few days I was forced to stay in bed. It was weeks before I was strong enough to do more than doze by the fireside, but at last I began to feel better. I was still too weak to walk outside, so I asked Nelly if she would come and sit with me, and continue her story where she had left off...

After Miss Cathy and Mr. Edgar were married, I went to live at Thrushcross Grange to help look after

Cathy. I was very sad to leave Wuthering Heights. My little Hareton was not yet five years old and I had just begun to teach him to read. It nearly broke my heart to leave the boy in that cheerless house, with only his drunken father and old Joseph to care for him.

Once she was settled in at the Grange, Cathy behaved a great deal better than I had expected. She seemed almost too fond of Mr. Edgar, and she even showed plenty of affection for his sister, Isabella. They certainly made a great fuss of her, bending over backwards to agree to all her wishes. I noticed that Edgar had a great fear of upsetting his wife, and none of the servants were allowed to answer her back or complain about her many orders.

I soon learned to respect my new master, with his kind and gentle ways. I even tried to be less touchy with Cathy in order to please him. For six months, we all lived peacefully together. There were times when Cathy was silent and gloomy, but Edgar was always understanding, believing that her spells of depression were caused by her long illness. When Cathy became cheerful again, Edgar was happy too, and it seemed to me then that they had a chance of deep and growing happiness. Perhaps such fragile happiness could never have lasted, but the way it came to an end was worse than anyone could have imagined.

One warm September evening, I was coming in from the garden with a basket of apples. The light was fading, and there were deep shadows on the grass. I had stopped by the kitchen door to look up at the moon, when I heard a voice behind me.

"Nelly, is that you?"

It was a man's voice – but not one I knew – although there was something familiar in the way he pronounced my name.

Something stirred outside the door, and, moving nearer, I saw a tall man in dark clothes with a dark face and hair. He leaned against the side of the porch, his fingers on the door latch, as if he were about to open it.

"Who can it be who knows my name?" I wondered, as I came closer.

"I've been waiting here for an hour," the voice continued, "and all the time the house has been as still as death. But don't you know who I am, Nelly? Take a look – I'm not a stranger."

I saw a face half-covered with whiskers and a pair of deep-set, glittering eyes... Of course, I remembered those eyes.

"What!" I cried in amazement, "Have you come back? Is it really you?"

"Yes, it's Heathcliff," he replied, impatiently, glancing up at the windows of the house. "Are they at home, Nelly? And where is your mistress? You needn't be so disturbed. I just want to have one word with her. Go and say that a person from Gimmerton is here and wishes to see her."

"But how will she take it?" I cried out. "What will she do? The shock of seeing you will send her out of her mind!"

"Go and carry my message," he interrupted. "I'm in torment until you do!"

Then he lifted the door latch for me and I entered the house.

When I reached the sitting room, I almost turned away. Edgar and Cathy were sitting by the fire, looking wonderfully peaceful in the evening light. I was about to leave them undisturbed, when something made me mutter, "A person from Gimmerton wishes to see you, madam."

"What does he want?" asked Cathy.

"I didn't question him."

"Well, close the curtains, Nelly, and bring us up some tea. I'll be back very soon."

After Cathy had left the room, Mr. Edgar asked carelessly who the visitor was.

"Someone the mistress doesn't expect," I replied. "It's that Heathcliff, you remember, who used to live at the Heights."

"What... the gypsy, the farm boy!" cried Edgar. "Why didn't you say so to Catherine?"

"Please sir, don't ever call him those names," I said. "My mistress will be so angry to hear them. You know she was heartbroken when Heathcliff ran off, and she'll be overjoyed to see him now."

Before long, I heard the click of the latch and Cathy flew into the room, breathless and wild, "Oh Edgar, Edgar darling," she panted, flinging her arms around his neck, "Heathcliff's come back!" And she tightened her hold to a squeeze.

"Well, well," said her husband, crossly, "don't strangle me for that! He never struck me as such a great treasure. There's no need to be so frantic."

"I know you didn't like him," she answered, trying to be calm, "but, for my sake, you must be friends now. Shall I ask him to come up?"

"Here?" he asked. "Into the sitting room?"

"Where else?"

"I would have thought the kitchen was more suitable for him."

Cathy gave him a strange look – half-laughing and half-cross.

"No," she said firmly. "I can't sit in the kitchen. Please set two tables here, Nelly – one for the grand folks – your master and Miss Isabella – and one for the commoners – Heathcliff and me. Oh, I must go and find him now!"

She was about to run off, when Edgar stopped her.

"Nelly will ask him to come in," he said. "And Catherine, try to be glad without being ridiculous. We don't want all the servants to see you welcoming a runaway farm boy as if he were your brother."

I went down to the porch and found Heathcliff waiting to be let in. He followed me in silence up the stairs and, as I showed him into the room, I managed to have a proper look at him. I was amazed to see just how much he had changed. He was now a tall, athletic man with a handsome, intelligent face. Beside him, my master Edgar looked like a pretty boy. He was very upright, which made me wonder if he had spent some time in the army. But whatever he'd been doing, this new Heathcliff dressed and acted like a gentleman – there were no signs of the ruffian he used to be. Only his eyes, I noticed, were still full of fire.

My master was also surprised to see how the farm boy had changed, and at first he didn't seem to know how to treat his guest. But Heathcliff just stood staring at Edgar, waiting coolly for him to speak.

"Sit down, sir," Edgar said, at last. "My wife wishes to welcome you into our home, and of course I am delighted when anything pleases her."

"And so am I," answered Heathcliff. "I shall gladly stay for an hour or two."

Then he took a seat opposite Cathy, who kept her eyes fixed on him all the time, as if she was afraid he would vanish any minute. Heathcliff didn't raise his eyes very often, but each time he did, I noticed his delight at seeing Cathy again.

The two of them were much too absorbed in each other to notice anyone else, but Edgar was pale with annoyance. This rapidly turned to anger when Cathy jumped up and seized both of Heathcliff's hands.

"Tomorrow, I shall think that this was all a dream!" she cried. "I shan't be able to believe that I've seen you and touched you again! And yet, cruel Heathcliff, you don't deserve this welcome… when you've been away for three whole years, and never thought of me!"

"A little more than you have thought of me!" he murmured. "Promise me you'll never drive me away again, Cathy. I've fought through a bitter life since I last saw you, and all my struggles have been only for you!"

"Catherine," interrupted Edgar, trying hard to stay calm, "please come to the table – we don't all want our tea to go cold. I'm sure Mr. Heathcliff has a long walk ahead of him and I, for one, am becoming thirsty."

Cathy took the teapot, and Miss Isabella arrived to join in the meal. But it hardly lasted ten minutes. Cathy's cup was never filled – she couldn't eat or drink, and Edgar managed to spill his tea and hardly swallowed a mouthful.

Heathcliff didn't stay much longer, and I was soon called to show him out. As he was on his way out, I asked if he was walking back to Gimmerton.

"No, to Wuthering Heights," he answered. "Hindley invited me there when I called on him this morning."

I was too amazed to reply. Hindley had invited Heathcliff... his old enemy? And Heathcliff had chosen to call on Hindley? What could he be plotting now? I thought about it long and hard after Heathcliff had gone, and the more I thought, the more worried I became. I had a heavy feeling in the bottom of my heart, and I wished for all our sakes that Heathcliff had stayed away.

Heathcliff moved into Wuthering Heights, and the news soon spread that he was staying up until all hours, playing cards and drinking with Mr. Hindley. I wondered what his plans could be, but I kept my fears to myself.

Meanwhile, Heathcliff began to pay visits to the Grange. But I noticed he was careful not to come too often or to stay too long, as if he were testing Edgar's patience. During these visits, Heathcliff said very little and Cathy managed to control her excitement, so Edgar began to feel that he could relax.

But Edgar soon had something new to worry about. After a few weeks of visits from Heathcliff, Isabella began to fall in love with him. She was now a charming young lady of eighteen, but with childish manners and a quick temper. Her brother loved her dearly and was horrified by her choice. He had the sense to realize that, although Heathcliff's appearance might have changed, he could never be trusted. Edgar felt and dreaded Heathcliff's savage power, and shrank from the thought of allowing his sister into its grasp.

We all noticed Miss Isabella's moods, and put up with her sighs and grumbles as well as we could. But one morning, Cathy couldn't bear it any longer. She insisted that Isabella should go to bed, while I went to fetch the doctor to see what was wrong.

"There's nothing wrong with me," sobbed Isabella. "It's just your cruelty that's making me unhappy!"

"When have I been cruel to you?" asked Cathy in amazement.

"Yesterday!" cried Isabella. "On our walk on the moor, you told me to go away while you talked to Heathcliff!"

"And that's your idea of cruelty? I simply thought that Heathcliff's talk was not very interesting to you."

"That's not the reason you sent me away," said Isabella. "You knew I wanted to be with him. But you had to keep him all to yourself!"

"You're an impertinent little monkey!" exclaimed Cathy in surprise. "But I don't believe this foolishness. Do you really want to be loved by Heathcliff? I hope I've misunderstood you, Isabella."

"No you haven't," Isabella insisted. "I love him more than you ever loved Edgar. And he might love me too, if only you'd let him."

"Well I wouldn't be you for a kingdom then! Nelly, tell Isabella what Heathcliff really is – a creature of stone and wildness, a fierce, pitiless, wolfish man. I'd rather let my tame canary out onto the stormy moors than allow you to fall in love with him. I know he couldn't love a Linton, but he'd marry you for your fortune and then crush you like a sparrow's egg. Listen to my advice, Isabella. I know Heathcliff and I'm speaking as his friend. Don't, whatever you do, fall into his trap."

Isabella looked at Cathy with horror. "You're a poisonous friend... you're worse than twenty enemies."

"Ah! You won't believe me then? You think I'm speaking from wicked selfishness?"

"I'm certain you are," flashed back Isabella, "and I shudder at you!"

"Good!" cried Cathy, leaving the room. "Try for yourself, if that's what you want. I won't argue with you any more."

I was left to comfort Isabella, but I was determined that she should be warned.

"Don't think about him any more, Miss Isabella," I said. "Your sister-in-law knows Heathcliff better than anyone else, and she would never pretend that he's worse than he is. Think about it carefully, Miss. Honest people don't keep their actions hidden, but what do we know about where he's been for these past three years? And what do you think he's doing up at the Heights? Why is he staying in the house of a man he despises? They say that Mr. Hindley is worse and worse since he came…"

"No, Nelly!" she interrupted. "You're as bad as Cathy and I won't listen to you. Why do you want to convince me there's no happiness in the world?"

Perhaps Isabella might have forgotten about Heathcliff if she'd been left to herself. But the next day, Edgar was out at a meeting all day, and Heathcliff arrived at the Grange very early. Cathy and Isabella were sitting in the library, and I noticed a smile cross Cathy's face when she saw Heathcliff arrive.

"Come in," she said cheerfully, "and let me congratulate you, Heathcliff. At last I've found someone who loves you more than I do. My poor sister-in-law is breaking her heart over you. You could become Edgar's brother! No, no, Isabella, you shan't run off," she continued, grasping the arm of the girl, who was trying to escape. "We were fighting like cats over you, Heathcliff, and Isabella told me that I must give you up, so she can make you hers forever!"

"Catherine," said Isabella, struggling to be free, "I'd thank you to stick to the truth! Mr. Heathcliff, please be kind enough to ask your friend to let me go."

Heathcliff did nothing to rescue Isabella, who was forced to free herself by using her nails.

"Well, there's a tigress!" exclaimed Cathy, setting her free, and shaking her hand with pain. "Now, run away Isabella and hide your vixen's face. How foolish of you to show those claws to him! Watch out Heathcliff, you must be careful of your eyes!"

"I'd wrench the nails off her fingers, if she ever used them on me," Heathcliff muttered brutally, when the door had closed behind Isabella. "But what are you doing teasing her like that, Cathy? You weren't speaking the truth were you?"

"I assure you I was," she replied. "She's been pining for you for weeks, and was raving about you yesterday. But take no more notice – I like her too much to let you devour her."

"And I like her too little to do it," replied Heathcliff. He was silent for a while, and then another thought struck him, "I believe that Isabella will inherit all her brother's wealth?" he asked slyly.

"You're much too interested in grasping other people's money," said Catherine angrily. "But let's forget all about it now."

Neither of them spoke about Isabella again, but I was sure that Heathcliff had not forgotten her. Several times, during the rest of the day, I noticed him smiling secretly to himself, and I decided that I would have to watch him very carefully. I was worried for Mr. Edgar, who was a kind and trusting man, and I longed to find a way to send Heathcliff away. His visits were a constant nightmare to me and, I suspected, to my master too. And as for his games up at the Heights – I dreaded to think where they would end. It seemed to me that we were like stray sheep, lost and alone, while a savage beast prowled around us, just waiting for the moment when he would spring.

Quarrels at the Grange

The next time Heathcliff came to Thrushcross Grange, Miss Isabella was in the garden, feeding the pigeons. She hadn't said a word to Cathy for days, but at least she'd stopped her complaining, which was a comfort to us all.

Usually, Heathcliff completely ignored Isabella. But this time he checked all the windows to see if anyone was watching, and then walked quickly over to her. I was standing by the kitchen window and saw it all. At first, Isabella seemed intent on getting away, but then I saw Heathcliff lay a hand on her arm. He asked her a question, and when she refused to answer, the scoundrel dared to take her in his arms!

"So now you're a cheat and a hypocrite as well!" I couldn't help saying out loud.

"Who is, Nelly?" said Cathy behind me – I hadn't noticed that she had come in.

"Your worthless friend!" I answered angrily. "What does he think he's doing with Miss Isabella?"

Cathy went out to meet Heathcliff, her eyes blazing.

"Why are you causing all this trouble?" she raged. "I thought you had promised to leave Isabella alone.

You'd better stop now or Edgar will lock you out of the house!"

"Just let him try!" growled Heathcliff. "I'm losing patience with him. Every day, I grow more desperate to see him gone!"

"For heavens' sake be quiet, or Edgar will hear you," said Cathy, closing the kitchen door. "Now why did you disobey me? Did Isabella fling herself at you?"

"What does it matter to you? She has every right to kiss me, and you have no right to object – I'm not your husband, so you needn't be jealous of me!"

"I'm not jealous of you," replied Cathy, crossly. "You're welcome to marry Isabella if you really like her. But tell me the truth, Heathcliff, do you really like her? I can't believe that you do."

"Who cares whether I like her or not?" replied Heathcliff coldly. "This has nothing to do with liking. And thank you for telling me Isabella's secret. I swear I'll make good use of it."

It was just as I feared – Heathcliff was going to trap Miss Isabella! I decided I had heard quite enough, and I hurried away to find my master.

"Nelly," Mr. Edgar said as I entered the room, "have you seen your mistress?"

"Yes, sir, she's in the kitchen, very upset by Mr. Heathcliff. And if you don't mind me saying so, sir, I think it's time to put an end to his visits."

Then I described what I'd seen in the garden, and the quarrel that followed, as much as I dared.

"This is unbearable!" Edgar stormed. "It's disgraceful that Catherine calls this man a friend and forces his company on me and my sister! Call some strong men to the kitchen, Nelly. I'll make sure my wife spends no more time with him!"

Edgar strode into the kitchen.

"Why are you still talking to this wretch, Catherine?" he began angrily. "You should have ordered him straight out of the house!"

"Have you been listening at the door, Edgar?" she replied mockingly, and Heathcliff added a sneering laugh.

My master kept very calm.

"Up until now, sir," he said quietly, "I have been very patient, but that time is over. Your presence is a poison that is spreading through my home, and I refuse to allow you to visit here again. In fact, if you don't leave in the next three minutes, I shall be forced to throw you out of my house!"

Heathcliff looked Edgar up and down with eyes full of scorn.

"Cathy, this little lamb of yours is threatening me like a bull!" he said. "The tiny creature is in danger of splitting its skull against my knuckles. Heavens, Linton, I'm sorry you're not worth the bother of knocking down!"

Edgar gave me a signal to get the men. But Cathy saw what was happening, and quickly locked the kitchen door, grabbing the key.

"Let's have a fair fight," she said to her husband. "If you don't have the courage to tackle Heathcliff on your own, you should apologize to him or let yourself be beaten. But don't pretend to be braver than you are. I'm not letting go of this key – and I hope that Heathcliff beats you thoroughly, as a punishment for daring to criticize me!"

Edgar tried to seize the key from Cathy, but she threw it into the hottest part of the fire. Then he sank back into a chair, overcome by shaking and his face deathly white.

"Oh, heavens!" said Cathy scornfully. "We are overcome! What a fine, brave knight you are! You're more like a baby rabbit than a lamb!"

"I wish you joy of this milk-blooded coward, Cathy," said Heathcliff roughly. "And this is the whimpering, shivering thing that you preferred to me! Is he weeping? Or is he going to faint from fear?"

Heathcliff gave Edgar's chair a little push, but this was enough. My master jumped up and punched him in the throat – a blow that would have flattened a smaller man. It took Heathcliff's breath away for a moment and, while he was choking, Edgar walked out of the back door and into the yard.

"There! That's the end of your visiting here," cried Cathy. "Get away now, before he comes back with a couple of pistols and half a dozen servants. Now, hurry up and go!"

"Do you think I'd leave now without crushing him into the ground?" roared Heathcliff.

"He's not coming back," I interrupted, inventing a story quickly. "But three men are coming up the path, and all of them are armed."

Heathcliff hesitated for a moment and then decided to leave. He seized a poker, smashed the lock on the kitchen door, and escaped through the house.

Cathy raced into the sitting room after him, but then clutched onto me, "I feel as if I'm losing my mind, Nelly!" she cried, throwing herself onto a sofa. "A thousand blacksmith's hammers are beating in my head! Tell Isabella to keep away – and tell Edgar I'm in danger of being seriously ill – I hope it will be true. He's upset me shockingly by daring to tell me what to do, and now I want to frighten him… But, Nelly, why don't you look more anxious about me?"

I'm sure my calmness was exasperating, but I believed that she should learn some self-control. I also didn't wish to frighten her husband any more. So I said nothing when I saw Edgar going to join her, but I took the liberty of listening at the door.

It was Edgar who spoke first.

"Stay where you are, Catherine," he said calmly, "I just want to know if you intend to continue your friendship with…"

"Oh, for heavens' sake," said Cathy, stamping her foot, "stop this lecturing now! I see your cold blood can't be worked up into a fever – your veins are full of ice water – but mine are boiling, and the sight of such chilliness makes them boil more!"

"If you want to get rid of the sight of me," Edgar continued, "you must answer my question. Will you give up Heathcliff or will you give me up instead? I need to know which of us you will choose."

"And I need to be left alone!" screamed Cathy. "Can't you see I can hardly stand? Leave me now, Edgar!"

Cathy rang the bell furiously until it broke with a twang. But I answered slowly. It was enough to try the patience of a saint, I thought, these wicked, senseless rages. There she lay, hitting her head against the arm of the sofa, and grinding her teeth as if she planned to break them into splinters. Mr. Edgar stood staring at her in a panic and told me to fetch some water as quickly as I could.

I brought a glass of water and, when Cathy wouldn't drink it, I sprinkled it over her face. In a few seconds, she stretched herself out stiff, her eyes rolled up and her cheeks turned deathly white. Edgar looked terrified.

"There's nothing the matter," I whispered. I didn't want him to be fooled by her play-acting, although I couldn't help feeling afraid.

"She has blood on her lips!" he said, shuddering.

"Never mind!" I answered sharply.

Suddenly, Cathy jumped up, her hair flying over her shoulders and her eyes flashing wildly. I was prepared for broken bones at least, but she only glared at me and then rushed upstairs. The master told me to follow her, but she locked herself in her room.

For the next few days, Miss Isabella moped around the garden, always silent and usually in tears. Her brother shut himself up in the library and tried to read his books, and Cathy stayed in her room, obstinately refusing to take any food. While all this was happening, I carried out my usual duties, convinced I was only sane person living at the Grange.

On the third day, Cathy unlocked her bedroom door and asked for a bowl of soup. She drank the soup eagerly, but then sank back onto her pillows, clenching her hands and groaning, "Oh, I will die, I'm sure I will die!"

"Did you want anything else, madam?" I asked, trying to stay calm in spite of her haggard appearance.

"What is Edgar doing?" she demanded, pushing her tangled hair away from her wasted face. "Is he ill too, or perhaps he is dead?"

"Neither," I replied calmly. "He's spending his time with his books, as he has no one else to talk to."

I know I shouldn't have spoken to Cathy like that, but I couldn't give up the idea that she was just pretending to be sick.

"With his books!" Cathy cried out, amazed. "While I am dying! Heavens, does he know how much I've changed?" She stared into the mirror. "Is that really Catherine Linton? Please tell him I'm not acting in a play. Does he care so little about my life?"

"No, madam," I answered, "the master has no idea that you are raging like this. And I don't think he's afraid that you will starve yourself to death."

"Do you think I won't, Nelly? Well then, tell him that I will. Say you have seen me and you're certain that I will."

"No, madam, you forget," I reminded her. "You've just had some soup and soon you'll be feeling better."

"Oh Nelly!" she interrupted. "Don't you care about me at all? You have no idea how tormented I've been. I've been haunted for these last few nights! But I begin to think you've all turned into my enemies. How dreary to die, surrounded by such cold faces!"

Then she began to rage, one minute tearing at her

pillow with her teeth, and the next leaping up and trying to open the window. The wild expression on her face and her rapid changes of mood began to frighten me. They reminded me of her earlier illness, and I decided I must fetch Mr. Edgar immediately.

One minute earlier, Cathy had been violent, but now she began to play with the feathers that escaped from her pillow and flew around the room.

"That's a turkey's," she murmured to herself, "and this is a wild duck's and that's a pigeon's. And here's a lapwing's. How I wish that I were a lapwing flying over the moor!"

"Stop playing like a baby!" I ordered, dragging the pillow away. But now she sat staring at the mirror.

"Do you see that face in the mirror, Nelly? What does it want from me?"

I told her it was her own face, but she refused to believe me, so in the end I covered it up with a shawl.

"It's still waiting there for me," she cried in terror. "Oh Nelly, this room is haunted, and I'm so frightened of being alone!"

"There's nobody here," I insisted, as I edged my way out of the room. But as I left the room I was summoned back by a piercing scream – the shawl had dropped off the mirror and she was petrified by what she saw.

"Now look in the mirror, madam," I said as firmly as I could, "and you'll see just yourself with me by your side."

Trembling and bewildered, she held onto me

tightly. "Oh Nelly… I hardly know where I am any more. I keep thinking I'm back at the Heights with Heathcliff, just after my father died. I wish I was a girl again, wild and free… and racing through the heather. If only I could feel the wind from the moors, I would be better. Just let me feel it, Nelly – let me have one breath."

I tried to stop her, but her delirious strength was much greater than mine, and she pushed open the window and leaned all the way out. Beyond the house, everything lay in misty darkness, but Cathy insisted she could see the lights at the Heights.

"Look, Nelly," she said eagerly, "there's my room with the candle in it and the trees swaying in front of

the window. And there's Joseph's lamp. He's waiting up late for me to come home so he can lock the gate. Well, he'll have to wait for a little while yet… it's a long journey over the moors and I must go past the graveyard to get there.

"Heathcliff and I used to play games in that

graveyard. But, Heathcliff, I dare you, will you come there now? I won't lie there all by myself. They can bury me twelve feet deep, but I won't rest until you're with me… I never will!"

At this moment, I heard the rattle of the doorlatch, and Mr. Edgar was in the room.

"Oh sir!" I cried, "my poor mistress is ill and I can't manage her at all. Please help me persuade her to go back to bed."

"Catherine ill?" he said, hurrying toward us. "Shut the window at once, Nelly! Catherine, my love, what has happened to you?"

"She's been sulking up here all on her own," I tried to explain. "And she's hardly eaten anything all that time. She wouldn't admit to any of this until this evening, so I couldn't tell you how she was. But please don't worry, sir. I'm sure it will pass…"

"So this is nothing is it, Nelly Dean?" my master said sternly. "You will need to explain yourself better than that!" Then he took his wife in his arms and stared at her in despair.

At first, Cathy didn't seem to recognize Edgar at all, but gradually she realized who he was. "Ah, so you've come at last, Edgar Linton," she said sadly. "I suppose there will be plenty of sorrowing now. But you can't keep me away from my narrow home on the moors… my resting place where I'll be before spring is over! That's where I'll be, not with the Lintons, under a church roof, but in the open air out in the churchyard, and you can please yourself, Edgar, whether you go to them or come to me!"

"Catherine, what's happened to you?" said Edgar, horrified. "Don't you care about me anymore? Do you love that wretch, Heath…"

"Stop!" cried Cathy. "Stop this minute. Don't mention that name, or I'll jump out of the window now. I don't want you any more, Edgar. I'm past wanting you… Go back to your books. I'm pleased you'll have them for company after I've gone."

"Her mind is wandering, sir," I interrupted. "She's been talking nonsense all evening. If you leave her quietly, I'm sure she'll get better. We'll just have to be careful not to upset her…"

"Thank you, Nelly," Mr. Edgar said coldly, "but I won't be needing any more advice from you. You never gave me a hint of how she's been these last few days! Months of sickness couldn't have caused such a change!"

I was covered with shame and confusion, and set off as fast as I could to find the doctor.

Isabella's story

As I was hurrying in the direction of the village, I thought I heard the sound of horses galloping down the lane. But I was too distracted to think about it then. It was only much later that I realized just what it meant.

Dr. Kenneth came straight back to the Grange with me. When he saw Cathy he was very worried. He was afraid she might not survive a second attack, and he told me secretly that, even if she lived, she could easily lose her mind.

I didn't close my eyes all night, and neither did Mr. Edgar. The next morning, the servants were up much earlier than usual and everyone in the house was busy except Miss Isabella. We were all surprised at how soundly she slept. But the mystery was solved when a maid came rushing into the room.

"Oh dear, oh dear, sir, whatever will happen next? It's Miss Isabella…"

"Speak quietly, Mary," said Edgar calmly. "Now tell me, what's your news? What is the matter with Miss Isabella?"

"She's gone, sir, she's gone! Mr. Heathcliff has run off with her!"

The maid had just come back from Gimmerton, where she'd heard a shocking story. At around midnight the night before, a gentleman and a lady had stopped to have a horse's shoe fixed a couple of miles outside the village. The blacksmith's daughter had recognized them both, but she'd waited until the morning to spread her news around the village.

"Should we try to bring them back, sir?" I asked my master.

"No, Nelly," he answered wearily. "Isabella has the right to go, if that's what she wanted. Don't trouble me about her any more. From now on, she is no longer my sister."

And that was all Edgar said on the subject. He didn't make any more inquiries, or even mention his sister's name, but concentrated all his love on Cathy.

Heathcliff and Isabella stayed away for two months and, during that time, Cathy survived the worst of her illness. No mother could have been more devoted to her child than Edgar was to his wife. He watched over her day and night, patiently suffering all her black moods and wild ravings. When, at last, she began to recover, she was very different from the girl we used to know. But Edgar was beside himself with joy that his beloved wife was out of danger.

The first time Cathy left her bedroom was early in March. Edgar placed a handful of crocuses on her pillow and she smiled with pleasure, for the first time in months.

"These are the earliest flowers from the Heights!" she said excitedly. "They remind me of spring winds and sunshine and nearly melted snow. Edgar, has the snow almost gone?"

"Yes, the snow has gone now, my dearest," he replied. "The sky is blue and the larks are singing. Oh Cathy, I wish I could take you onto the moors. I believe that it would cure you!"

"I shall only be there once more," said the invalid, "and then you must leave me and I'll stay there forever. Next spring, you'll look back and think you were happy today."

Edgar tried to cheer her up with kind words and kisses, but Cathy just let the tears roll down her cheeks.

My master told me to light a fire downstairs and put a chair by the window in the sunshine. Then he carried Cathy downstairs, and she sat for a long while, enjoying the gentle warmth. We began to hope, at last, that she might recover. And there was a double reason for us to be hopeful, because she was expecting a baby in the summer.

At about this time, I received a letter from Miss Isabella, who had returned to Wuthering Heights. It was not at all the sort of letter you might expect to receive from a bride who had only just returned from her honeymoon.

Dear Nelly,

I came to Wuthering Heights last night and heard for the first time that Cathy has been very ill. I suppose I mustn't write to her, and Edgar refuses to have anything to do with me. So the only person left to write to is you.

Please tell Edgar that I'd give anything to see his dear face again, and that my heart returned to Thrushcross Grange within a day of leaving it. It is there now, full of warm feelings for him and Cathy.

And now I have a question for you... Is Heathcliff really a man and, if so, is he insane? Don't write to me, Nelly – your letter won't get through – but please come and visit me here as soon as possible, and bring me some sign that Edgar has forgiven me.

I won't bother to tell you about the lack of comforts at Wuthering Heights – that is the least of my problems. And as for my companions, little Hareton does nothing but swear and kick at me, and Hindley is a wreck of a man. There are no servants here except for surly old Joseph, and no room I can call my own. Heathcliff keeps his bedroom locked, and Hindley tries the door every night, hoping that it might be unlocked so he can blow out Heathcliff's brains while he sleeps. I must admit that when I saw Hindley's rifle, I wished that I had a weapon too!

Truly, Nelly, this is a madhouse. I hate and fear my husband, and I am completely desperate. My only hope is that you will come and visit me here. I will look out for you every day – so please don't disappoint me!

Isabella

As soon as I'd finished reading Isabella's letter, I went straight to my master and told him his sister's news. I asked if I could visit her and send her a sign of his forgiveness, but he wouldn't give in.

"You can call at Wuthering Heights if you like," Edgar said sadly, "and tell Isabella that I am not angry, but sorry to have lost her. But I won't be seeing her again. We are divided forever."

"Won't you even write her a note, sir?"

"No, Nelly, I can't do that. I won't have anything to do with the Heathcliff family. So far as I'm concerned, it doesn't exist."

Mr. Edgar's coldness depressed me greatly, and all the way across the moors I tried to think of a way to comfort Miss Isabella. As I approached the Heights, I saw her looking out of the window, but when I waved to her, she drew back immediately, as if she was afraid of being seen.

I walked straight into the house without knocking. The place was dismal and dreary compared with the home I had left a couple of years before. Hindley was out and Hareton was nowhere to be seen, but Heathcliff was sitting at a table, working on some papers. He stood up when I came in and offered me a chair. He was the only thing in the house that looked at all decent, and I thought that he had never looked better. But Isabella did not look good – her dress was dirty and her hair hung down in greasy strands around her face. Anyone who didn't know them would have thought that Heathcliff was the master and she was his servant.

Isabella ran forward eagerly to meet me, holding out her hand for a letter from Edgar. I shook my head, but she followed me to the sideboard and started whispering to me. Meanwhile, Heathcliff had seen what was happening.

"Nelly, if you've anything for Isabella, give it to her now. We don't have any secrets here."

"I have nothing, sir," I said, thinking it was best to tell the truth. "My master told me to tell his sister not to expect a letter or a visit from him. He sends his love, madam, and his good wishes for your happiness, but he says there can be no contact between his household and yours."

Isabella's lip quivered slightly and she returned to her seat by the window. Her husband stood in front of the fire and started to question me.

"Now, Nelly, tell me, how is Cathy?"

I told him as little as I could about her illness.

"She's recovering slowly now, sir, but she'll never be the same as she was, and if you have any feelings for her you'll keep well away."

"You know I'll never be able to keep away from her," he replied. "And you must promise, Nelly, to find a way to let me see her soon."

"I'll make no promises to you, Heathcliff. You must not see her – another meeting between you and Edgar would kill her!"

"With your help that could be avoided," he said slyly.

"No, you will not disturb her now, just as she's finding some peace and has nearly forgotten you."

"Do you really think that she has forgotten me?" he said. "Oh, Nelly! You must know that she hasn't. You know as well as I do that she thinks of me a thousand times more than she thinks of Edgar. He is hardly any dearer to her than her dog or her horse. It's just not possible for him to love like me."

"Cathy and Edgar are as fond of each other as any two people can be!" interrupted Isabella. "No one has a right to talk about my brother that way!"

"Your brother is wonderfully fond of you too, isn't he?" observed Heathcliff cruelly. "I see he's quite happy to turn you out into the world."

"He doesn't know what I suffer," Isabella replied. "I didn't tell him that."

"My lady is looking sadly the worse for her marriage," I dared to say, "somebody here clearly doesn't know how to love."

"It's her own fault," Heathcliff answered scornfully. "As you can see, she makes no effort at all to please me. But she suits my house better by not being too ladylike, and I'll make sure she doesn't disgrace me by wandering around outside."

"Well, sir," I insisted, "Miss Isabella is used to having servants to care for her. She should have a maid to look after her and you should treat her more kindly."

"I'll treat her how I please!" thundered Heathcliff. "You wouldn't believe, Nelly, what a pitiful, quivering creature she is. She doesn't even have the courage to kill me, even though I know she would dearly love to!" He turned to his wife. "Go upstairs, child," he ordered her, "I've something to say to Nelly on her own."

I started to put on my bonnet, not wanting to hear any more from Heathcliff, but he shouted at me, "Put that down, Nelly! Either I'll persuade you to let me see Cathy, or I'll have to force you to do it. I swear I won't do her any harm — I just need to see her and know how she is.

"Last night, I was in the Grange garden, waiting under Cathy's window for six long hours, and I'll return there tonight and every night until I'm let in. If Edgar tries to stop me, I won't hesitate to knock him down, and if any servant dares to get in my way I'll shoot at them with my pistol. But wouldn't it be better to arrange a peaceful meeting? And you could do it so easily, Nelly! I'd warn you when I came, and you could let me in secretly and wait until I left. Then you wouldn't be doing any harm."

I protested that the shock of seeing him would be more than Cathy could bear. "She's all nerves, sir, and the shock could kill her. I'm serious, Heathcliff, and if you insist on seeing her, I shall be forced to tell my master so he can stop you."

"Then I shall be forced to keep you prisoner here," cried Heathcliff. "Nelly, you will not leave Wuthering Heights until you agree."

Well, I argued and complained and flatly refused fifty times, but in the end I had to give in. Heathcliff made me take a letter to Cathy and promise to let him know when Edgar was next away.

Was I right or was I wrong? I'm very much afraid that I was wrong, as the rest of my story will show.

Births and deaths

I kept Heathcliff's letter safe in my pocket, waiting for a time when my master was out. But it was four days later when I finally saw my chance. Mr. Edgar and the rest of the servants set off to walk to church, and I was left alone in the house with my mistress.

Cathy sat by an open window, enjoying the warm spring sunshine. Her appearance was greatly changed since her illness, and there was a strange, unearthly beauty in her face. Her once-flashing eyes were dreamy and melancholy, and she seemed to be always gazing into the distance – as if she were looking at something beyond this world.

"Here's a letter for you, madam," I said, putting it into her lifeless hand. "You must read it now, because it needs an answer. Shall I open it for you?"

"Yes, Nelly," she answered, but then she let it fall. I gave it back to her.

"Shall I read it for you, madam? It's from Mr. Heathcliff."

She looked startled.

"He says he wishes to see you," I said as gently as I could, "and he's in the garden now, waiting for your answer."

As I spoke, we heard footsteps in the hall. Cathy bent forward, listening breathlessly, and a minute later Heathcliff had found the door. In just two strides he was at Cathy's side, and had grasped her in his arms.

For five whole minutes, Heathcliff held Cathy in silence, covering her with kisses, and I saw he could hardly bear to look at her face. He had seen immediately that she would never recover, and was sure to die very soon.

"Oh, Cathy! Oh, my life! How can I bear it?" he cried out in despair.

"What?" said Cathy, leaning back weakly. "Am I meant to pity you now? You and Edgar have both treated me so cruelly — you've broken my heart. Together you have killed me, but you will go on living. See how strong you are, Heathcliff! How many years do you plan to live after I am dead? Will you forget me and be happy when I am in my grave?"

"Oh, Cathy, please don't torture me like this," he cried, grinding his teeth. "How can you talk to me like this when I can see that you're dying? Don't you realize your words will be burned forever into my memory, after you've left me and you are at peace?"

"I shall never be at peace," moaned Cathy. "How can I be at peace if we are parted?"

Heathcliff could bear it no longer, and he walked away from Cathy, his chest heaving with emotion. So she turned to me instead.

"Oh, Nelly, I'm so tired of this prison. I'm longing to escape to a different, glorious world. And soon I shall be there. Then I'll be beyond and above you all. But now I want to be with Heathcliff... Heathcliff, won't you please come to me now?"

Cathy tried to stand up, and Heathcliff turned towards her, his eyes wild and wet. For a moment they stood apart, then Cathy made a wild leap at Heathcliff. He just managed to catch her and they fell into each other's arms, locked tightly together as though they would never part.

"Why have you been so cruel to me, Cathy?" said Heathcliff wildly. "Why did you marry Edgar when it was me that you loved? If we had been together, nothing would have parted us, but you chose to do this. I haven't broken your heart — it's you who has broken it! And you've broken mine as well. Do you think I want to live after you've gone? What kind of living will it be when you are in your grave?"

"If I've done wrong, I'm dying for it now," sobbed Cathy. "But you left me too, Heathcliff. And I'll forgive you, if you forgive me now!"

"It's hard to forgive you, and look in your sunken eyes. Kiss me again, Cathy, but don't let me see your eyes!"

Then they were silent and clung to each other, drenched in each other's tears.

Suddenly, I noticed through the window a group of people walking home from church.

"My master will be here very soon," I warned them. But they never moved.

Soon I saw Edgar opening the garden gate.

"Now he's here," I cried. "For heaven's sake, hurry! If you go now, you can still miss him."

"I must go, Cathy," said Heathcliff, "but I'll stay close to your window."

"No! You mustn't go!" she shrieked. "It's the last time! Edgar can't hurt us, Heathcliff. I shall die if you go!"

At that moment, Edgar opened the door. He rushed towards Heathcliff, shaking with rage. But before Edgar could reach him, Heathcliff had stepped forward.

"Look after Cathy first," he said, putting her lifeless body into her husband's arms, "and then you can speak to me!"

Cathy lay unconscious in Edgar's arms, and while we tried desperately to revive her, Heathcliff crept silently out into the garden. Eventually, Cathy came around, but all she could do was sigh and moan and look around her wildly, not recognizing us at all. We put her straight to bed, and around midnight her baby was born, two months early. A couple of hours later, Cathy died, without ever recovering consciousness enough to see her daughter.

Edgar was so desperate with grief that he completely ignored his child, who we named Catherine after her mother. It seemed a terrible start for the puny little thing, and I worried that she had a difficult future ahead of her. The Lintons' fortune was oddly arranged so that all Edgar's wealth and property would go to Isabella after his death. If Edgar died, Isabella and Heathcliff would inherit everything, and little Catherine would be left with nothing.

Finally, morning came, and Edgar fell asleep, worn out with grief. I went out to look for Heathcliff and found him leaning on an old ash tree, his hair soaked in dew. When he saw me coming, he raised his eyes to me.

"She's dead!" he said. "You needn't tell me that. And put your handkerchief away, Nelly – she doesn't want your tears!"

"Yes, she's dead!" I answered, trying to stop my sobs.

"Tell me, Nelly," he urged, "how did she… ?" He struggled to speak, trembling all over. "How did she die?" he managed to say at last.

"As quietly as a lamb," I answered. "She died in a

gentle dream – and may she wake as gently in heaven!"

"May she wake in torment!" he cried out violently. "Catherine Earnshaw, may you not rest as long as I am living! You said that I killed you – well haunt me, then! Be with me always – take any form – drive me insane! Only don't leave me in this darkness where I cannot find you! You know I can't live without my life! I can't live without my soul!"

Then he started beating his head against the tree trunk and howling like a savage beast in pain.

Cathy was buried in Gimmerton churchyard five days later. Edgar spent every night until then sitting by her coffin, while Heathcliff kept watch in the garden outside. On the day of her funeral, only Edgar and the servants accompanied Cathy's coffin to her grave. To my surprise, she wasn't buried inside the church with the Lintons, or with her parents by the church door. Instead, her grave was dug on a green slope in the corner of the churchyard, just where the graveyard meets the moor.

On the evening of Cathy's funeral, the warm spring sunshine changed to snow. Soon the primroses were covered in wintry snowdrifts and the larks were silent again. The mood in the Grange was dismal. My master stayed in his study while I took over the sitting room, turning it into a nursery for baby Catherine. I spent my days trying to comfort the tiny moaning doll of a child, and watching the sleet and snow driving outside.

The day after the funeral, I was sitting with the baby, when the door opened and I heard a familiar voice. It was Isabella Heathcliff and she was in a terrible state.

"Don't be scared, Nelly, it's only me!" she panted, "I've run all the way from Wuthering Heights, and I can't count the number of falls I've had. Oh, I'm aching all over, but I can't stay. I just need to collect a few clothes and then take a carriage on to Gimmerton."

Her hair and clothes were dripping wet, and all she was wearing was a short-sleeved dress and a thin pair of shoes. She had a deep cut under one ear, and her face was covered in scratches and bruises. I also noticed that she was expecting a baby.

"My dear young lady," I exclaimed, "you must at least get warm and dry and let me bandage your wound, before you go any further."

She agreed to rest by the fire for a few minutes and, while I was looking after her, she told me her sad story...

"I daren't stay long," she began, "or Heathcliff will find me and force me to go back to the Heights. He was in such a fury when I left! I wish I could stay to comfort Edgar and help you with the baby, but Heathcliff would never allow it. He hates me with a passion and he loves to make me suffer. I can't believe I ever liked him. How could Cathy have loved such a monster?"

"Hush! He's a human being," I said. "There are worse men than him!"

"He's not a human being," she replied, "he's a fiend! And I can't feel sorry for him now, not if he wept tears of blood for Cathy. But you ask me why I left…

"Yesterday, you know, was the day of Cathy's funeral, and Heathcliff came back after six days away, looking like a savage wolf with his cannibal teeth gleaming in the dark. That night, Hindley tried to shoot Heathcliff with his rifle, and he would have succeeded if only Heathcliff hadn't been so strong. Heathcliff didn't stop beating Hindley until he was black and blue, and I just watched it all and wished I had the strength to overpower the brute myself.

"The next morning I decided it was time for my revenge. I waited until Hindley was prowling around the house, ready to pay Heathcliff back for the night before. Then I began to torment my husband in the best way I knew – by telling him that he could never have made Cathy happy! This made him so wild that he threw a knife at me, which cut me in the neck, and I ran screaming out of the kitchen. Hindley heard the scream and leaped on Heathcliff. Then I left them fighting like bears and ran all the way here!"

Isabella stopped her story. The carriage had arrived to take her to Gimmerton and she was anxious to be gone. Before she left, she kissed Edgar's and Cathy's portraits, and scooped her little dog up into her arms.

I believe she settled somewhere near London, and a few months later she had a son. She and Edgar wrote to each other regularly, but Isabella never came to Yorkshire again.

Somehow, Heathcliff learned from the servants about his son. Once, when I saw him in the village, he stopped and spoke to me.

"I hear Isabella's called my son Linton. She must want me to hate him too!"

"I don't think she wants you to know anything about him," I replied frostily.

"Well, she can keep him now," he said grimly. "But one day I'll have him, she can be sure of that!"

After Cathy's death, my master was a changed man. He almost never left the Grange except to visit Cathy's grave. But he did have one great comfort in life – his little daughter Catherine. He soon stopped neglecting her and became immensely fond of the child, spending most of his days playing and talking with her.

I sometimes used to compare Edgar with Hindley, and wonder to myself how these two men could have turned out so differently. Both of them had lost a wife they adored and both had a child to care for. But Hindley, who had always seemed the stronger of the two to me, allowed himself to fall apart, while Edgar devoted himself to being a good father.

Poor Hindley died soon after his sister. We never found out exactly what happened to him, but the doctor said he had drunk himself to death. By the time Hindley died, he had nothing to leave to his son. Heathcliff had won his house and all his money by playing him at cards. And young Hareton, who should have inherited Wuthering Heights, was forced to work as a servant for his father's enemy. The cuckoo had finally taken over the nest.

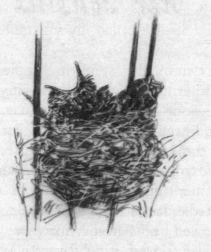

Catherine and her cousins

The next twelve years were the happiest of my life. Young Catherine was such a lively, affectionate little girl that no one close to her could stay sad for long. She was a beautiful child, with the Earnshaws' dark eyes and the Lintons' delicate features and golden hair. I have to admit that she had her faults – she had inherited her mother's temper, and hated being contradicted, but she was so loveable that we almost always allowed her to have her own way.

Mr. Edgar and his daughter were very close. He was her only teacher, and she was such a fast learner that her lessons were a pleasure for them both. Until Catherine was thirteen, she had never been beyond the walls of Thrushcross Park, except for short walks with her father, or to go to church. As far as she knew, Mr. Heathcliff and Wuthering Heights simply didn't exist. She and her father lived like hermits and, for a long while, she seemed perfectly happy with her isolated life.

Then, one evening, I noticed Catherine looking out over the moors.

"Nelly, how long will it be before I can walk to the top of those hills?" she asked. "I wish I knew what lies on the other side of them – is it the sea?"

"No, Miss Catherine. It's hills again, just like these."

"And how does it feel to stand under those golden rocks?" she said, pointing up to Peniston Crags.

"They're not so wonderful as they look from down here, miss," I said firmly, "and the hill on which they stand is very hard to climb."

"Oh, so you've been up there!" she cried excitedly. "And can I go too, when I'm older? Has papa climbed up to those rocks as well?"

"Your father would tell you that they're not worth visiting. The fields where you walk with him are much nicer, and Thrushcross Park is the finest place in the world."

"But I know every bit of the park," she murmured to herself, "and I would love to see the view from those hills. I'm sure my pony Minny could take me there easily."

Once she'd started to dream about Peniston Crags,

young Catherine wouldn't let the idea drop. She begged her father again and again to take her up to the Crags, and every few months she would ask him the same question, "Now, am I old enough to climb to the Crags?"

Edgar dreaded the thought of his precious daughter passing close to Wuthering Heights, so he kept giving the answer, "Not yet, my love, not yet."

Isabella Heathcliff lived for twelve years after leaving her husband. None of the Lintons were strong, and I believe she died from a kind of fever. Before she died, she wrote to her brother begging him to visit her in London. She wanted to say goodbye, and to hand over her son Linton to him. Even though Edgar hated leaving home, he immediately set off for London and left me in charge of Catherine, repeating his orders that she must not be allowed to leave the park.

Edgar was away for three weeks. For the first few days, Catherine sat in a corner of the library, too sad to play or even to read a book, but she soon became bored and restless. I was much too busy to look after her all day, so I told her to go out for a ride on her pony, never imagining that she would leave the park. Catherine asked me to pack a picnic for her so she could stay out all day. Then she set off on her pony with the dogs running behind her. I told her to ride carefully and be back soon after lunch, but the naughty thing never appeared for her tea.

I set out to find her, but when I reached the park

gates, a workman told me he'd seen her jumping the wall and galloping out of sight.

I was sure that Catherine was heading for Peniston Crags. I covered the miles as fast as I could and, after about an hour of heavy climbing, I reached the path that led to Wuthering Heights. The Crags were still a mile and a half beyond the house, and I began to be afraid that it would be completely dark before I reached them.

"What if she tried to climb the rocks," I thought to myself, "and slipped and broke her leg?" I was becoming desperate when I noticed, to my great relief, one of Miss Catherine's dogs running out of the farmhouse to meet me.

I raced up to the house and hammered on the door, which was opened by Zillah, the housemaid at the Heights.

"Ah," she said, " I see you've come for your little mistress! Don't be frightened. She's here, safe and sound."

"And is Heathcliff at home?" I panted, breathless with fear.

"No, no," she replied. "He won't be back for an hour or more. Come in and rest for a while."

I entered the room and saw my precious Catherine, sitting on a rocking chair that used to be her mother's. She seemed perfectly at home, and was laughing and talking to Hareton, who was now a strong, handsome lad of eighteen. He was staring at her, open-mouthed with astonishment, as she chattered away to him cheerfully.

"Well, miss!" I said, as sternly as I could. "This is your last ride until your papa comes back. I won't trust you outside the house again, you naughty, naughty girl!"

"But, Nelly!" she cried, ignoring my bad temper. "I've had such a great adventure. Have you ever been here in your life before?"

"Put on your hat and come home at once," I said firmly. "I'm very cross with you, Miss Catherine. What do you think your father will say when he hears you've been sneaking off like this!"

"But what have I done?" she sobbed. "Papa won't be angry with me. He's never cross, like you!"

"Come on," I repeated. "Let's get away now."

But Catherine had dodged away from me and was skipping around the room, hiding behind the furniture. Hareton was laughing, and Catherine was growing more and more impertinent.

"Well, Miss Catherine," I cried out in anger, "if you only knew whose house this was you'd be glad enough to leave."

"It's your father's, isn't it?" she said, turning to Hareton.

"No," he replied, looking down sulkily.

"Whose then – your master's?"

He swore and turned away.

"Nelly, who is this boy?" she said, turning to me. "He talked about 'our house' so I thought he must be the owner's son. But if he's a servant he should call me 'miss', shouldn't he?"

This made Hareton turn as black as a thundercloud.

"Now, go and get my horse," Catherine said, ordering Hareton around as if he were a stable boy. "What's the matter with you? Get my horse, I say."

"You saucy witch, I won't be your servant!" Hareton growled.

Catherine stared at him in astonishment. "How dare you speak to me like that? Why don't you do as I tell you!"

"Now, miss," interrupted Zillah, "you really should treat him better than that. Mr. Hareton is your cousin, and it's not his job to serve you."

"He can't be my cousin!" Catherine cried, with a scornful laugh. "Papa has just gone to London to fetch my cousin and he's a gentleman's son, not a farm boy like him!"

I was very angry with Catherine and Zillah. Now Heathcliff would be bound to hear that Linton was coming to live at the Grange, and Catherine would be sure to ask her father about Hareton. On our walk back to the Grange, I explained to Catherine that if her father discovered she had been up at the Heights, he might be so angry with me that he would send me away. The dear girl couldn't bear to think of that, so she promised to keep quiet about her adventures on the moors.

A few days later, we heard from Mr. Edgar that he was coming home and bringing Linton with him.

Catherine was wild with joy at the idea of welcoming her father back, and meeting her 'real' cousin. She couldn't wait to have someone of her own age to play with.

But, when the carriage arrived, Linton stayed huddled in the corner and took no notice of his excited cousin. He was a pale, delicate-looking boy – very much like his uncle at the same age, but with a sickly, peevish expression that Edgar had never had. Even though it was summer, he was wrapped in a warm, fur-lined cloak, and he shrank away from Catherine, whining that he just wanted to go to bed.

Edgar carried Linton into the house and sat him on a chair, where he immediately started to cry again.

"I can't sit on that chair," he sobbed. "It's much too hard."

"Lie on the sofa, then, and Nelly will bring you some tea," his uncle answered patiently.

Catherine pulled up a footstool and sat beside her cousin. At first she was silent, trying not to trouble him, but soon she decided to make a pet of him, and started stroking his curls and kissing his cheeks and offering him tea in a saucer, just like a baby. This pleased the feeble boy, who dried his eyes and gave a faint smile.

"This will be good for the boy," Edgar said cheerfully. "And he'll soon grow stronger, with another child to keep him company."

"If only we can keep him with us!" I thought to myself.

Later that evening, old Joseph arrived from
Wuthering Heights and asked to speak to my master.

"Heathcliff has sent for his lad," he announced,
"and I must bring him back with me tonight."

Edgar was silent for a moment. He wanted to do
his best to protect his sister's child, but he knew he
couldn't refuse Linton's father.

"Tell Mr. Heathcliff," he said, "that his son will
come to Wuthering Heights tomorrow. He's in bed

119

now and I won't let him go till the morning."

"No!" shouted Joseph, thumping the table. "I must take him with me now!"

"You won't take him tonight," answered Edgar firmly. "Now go and tell your master what I said."

"Very well!" growled Joseph, as he left the room. "But if you don't send the lad tomorrow, Heathcliff will come himself and take him home."

At five o'clock the next morning, I went in to wake young Linton. He was very unhappy at the thought of another journey, but I tried to comfort him by telling him how excited his father was to meet him.

"My father!" he cried in amazement. "Mama never told me I had a father. I'd much rather stay here with Uncle Edgar."

Eventually, I persuaded him to come with me, and we set off on horseback across the moors. All the way there, Linton kept asking me questions about his father, and I struggled to answer him as truthfully as I dared.

When we arrived at Wuthering Heights, Heathcliff, Joseph and Hareton all came out of the house to stare at Linton.

"Surely," said Joseph, "that can't be a boy? Mr. Edgar's sent you a girl instead!"

Heathcliff gave a scornful laugh. "My God! What a beauty! What a lovely, charming thing! This is even worse than I expected!"

I helped the trembling boy down from his horse,

and he clung to me and sobbed, but Heathcliff dragged him roughly away.

"I hope you'll be kind to him," I told Heathcliff fiercely, "or he won't live long. And he's the only family you have in the world."

"Oh, I'll look after him, don't you worry," he replied, laughing. "I want him to inherit Thrushcross Grange one day. And I'll make sure he's brought up like a gentleman. But I can't say I'll be proud of such a pale-faced, whining wretch!"

So I left poor Linton up at the Heights, and returned home sadly, not knowing when I'd see him again. Miss Catherine was bitterly disappointed to find that her young cousin had gone to stay with his father, and for a few weeks she asked about him every day. But eventually she forgot all about him, and life at the Grange returned to normal.

Whenever I saw Zillah in Gimmerton, I asked her about Linton. She told me he was often ill and always complaining. Heathcliff despised his son for being such a weakling, and hated the way he looked like Edgar. But he obviously had a plan for the boy. Zillah was given instructions to feed him only the finest food and to give him all the books he wanted.

Meanwhile, down at the Grange, life continued peacefully until Miss Catherine was sixteen years old. We never celebrated her birthday, because it was also the day that her mother had died. Mr. Edgar always spent the day alone, and Catherine was left to please herself. So, on the morning of her sixteenth birthday, she came downstairs ready for a walk on the moors with me.

It was a beautiful spring day, and I was happy to enjoy the sunshine while Catherine bounded ahead of me, searching for a moorhen's nest in the heather.

Before I realized it, we were nearly up at the Heights. I called to her to turn back, but she was too far away to hear me, and when I caught up with her at last, I saw she was talking to two men. I recognized them immediately as Heathcliff and Hareton.

"Miss Catherine," I panted, "we must go home immediately."

But Catherine refused. "This gentleman has asked me to go back to his house and meet his son. He says I've met him before, but I don't think that can be right, do you?"

And before I could stop her, Catherine was off, scampering towards the house with Hareton running after her.

"Heathcliff, this is very wrong," I said to him angrily. "You know Mr. Edgar will be furious if

Catherine sees Linton again."

"But I want her to see Linton," Heathcliff replied. "It's part of my plan. I want the two cousins to fall in love and marry. Then Catherine will inherit the Grange with Linton – now isn't that a generous plan?"

"And if they marry, but Linton dies," I asked, "would Catherine then inherit the Grange?"

"No, she would not. My son's property would go to me, but it still suits me to see them married."

I was very angry with Heathcliff, and afraid for Catherine, but by now we had reached the Heights and it was too late.

Linton was standing in front of the fire.

"Now, who's that?" asked Mr. Heathcliff, turning to Catherine. "Can you tell?"

"Your son?" she asked doubtfully.

"Yes, yes," he answered, "but don't you remember seeing him before? Linton, I'm sure you remember your cousin – you were always asking to see her!"

"What, Linton?" cried Catherine joyfully. "Is that little Linton? He's taller than I am now! Are you really Linton?"

The boy stepped forward and they both gazed at each other in wonder. Catherine had become a real beauty, sparkling with health and fun, and Linton was tall and graceful-looking, but very pale and thin.

Catherine turned to Heathcliff. "So you must be my uncle! Why don't you ever visit us at the Grange?"

"I visited it once too often before you were born," he answered. "Your father and I had a terrible argument, and now he hates me. If you say you've been here, he'll never let you come again."

"Well, if I'm not allowed here, then Linton can come to the Grange," said Catherine happily.

"It'll be too far for me," whined her cousin. "It would kill me to walk four miles."

Heathcliff looked scornfully at his son.

"I'm afraid my plan will never work," he muttered to me. "How could Catherine fall in love with a weakling like him?"

Linton certainly seemed a selfish, feeble boy. He refused to show his cousin around the farm, so Hareton gladly took the job instead.

While Catherine and Hareton were out, and Linton was huddled over the fire, Heathcliff revealed some more of his feelings to me.

"All my life I've wanted to have my revenge on Hindley for treating me so badly when I was young. And now I've done it. His son Hareton is as rough and sullen as I used to be. Or even worse... because he can't even read his own name!

"But I can't help seeing that Hareton is a son to be proud of, while my son is just a weak, moaning baby. But at least Linton is a gentleman. He will be rich and marry Catherine, and then I will enjoy watching him make her wretched. I want to make Edgar's daughter suffer, and my selfish son will certainly do that job for me."

While we were talking, Linton had gone to join Catherine and Hareton outside, and I could hear the two younger ones laughing at Hareton for his rough way of talking. As I listened to Linton mocking Hareton, I began to feel less sorry for him and even started to dislike the boy.

The next day, Catherine told her father all about our visit. He was very distressed by the news and warned her to keep well away from the Heights. Edgar was afraid that Catherine might be in danger from one of Heathcliff's plots. But he hated to talk about Heathcliff, so he didn't explain any of his fears to her. When Catherine begged her father to let her visit Linton, he refused to allow it, and this made her puzzled and upset.

Over the next few weeks, I noticed that Catherine had become very fond of sneaking off into corners to read by herself. She started getting up early and hanging around the kitchen when the milk was being delivered, and she had a drawer full of papers, which she kept locked up all the time.

In the end, I decided I had better find out what was happening. So one day, while Catherine was out, I found a key to open her drawer, and pulled out a pile of letters. I was horrified to see that they were love letters from Linton – shy and embarrassed at first, but then becoming more passionate, and some of them clearly written by Heathcliff. The two cousins had been writing to each other for weeks, and Catherine had been using the milk delivery boy as their messenger.

As soon as I could, I asked Miss Catherine about the letters. She sobbed and sulked, and said that she really loved Linton, but I was not impressed.

"Do you call that love?" I cried scornfully. "I've never heard anything so stupid! I might just as well talk of loving the miller who comes once a year to buy our corn. You've hardly seen Linton for more than four hours in your life!"

After a lot of argument, Catherine finally agreed not to write any more, and we burned the letters together. The next morning I sent a very different message to young Linton.

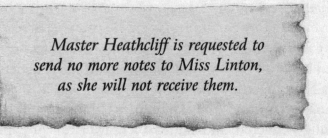

Master Heathcliff is requested to send no more notes to Miss Linton, as she will not receive them.

I sincerely hoped that this would be the last we heard of Linton.

Heathcliff's revenge

That summer, Mr. Edgar caught a bad cold, which developed into pneumonia, and he was forced to stay indoors for most of the winter. Poor Catherine missed her walks with her father, and I could see that she was feeling sad and restless.

One day, we were walking in Thrushcross Park when I noticed she was crying.

"What's the matter, Miss Catherine?" I asked.

"Oh Nelly, I'm thinking how sad and lonely I'd be if papa dies."

"Now, miss, you mustn't think like that," I said firmly. "I'm sure your father has many happy years ahead of him. Just you make certain you don't do anything to upset him, and he is sure to recover soon."

We walked on for about an hour, but just as we were arriving back at our gate, a man on a horse came riding by. I recognized him immediately. It was Heathcliff.

"Miss Linton!" he called out. "I'm very glad to meet you. Please don't rush away."

"I won't speak to you, Mr. Heathcliff," answered Catherine. "Papa says I must have nothing to do with you."

"It's my son I've come about, not me. You've played a cruel trick on him – first sending him love letters and then plunging him into despair. In fact, he's so miserable now that I think he's going to die. He'll be dead before the summer unless you can help him!"

"How can you lie to her like that?" I called out crossly. "Miss Catherine, don't listen to his nonsense. No one can die of love for a stranger."

"I swear Linton is dying," repeated Heathcliff solemnly. "Come and visit him next week and bring Nelly with you. I shall be away, so your father won't be angry with you."

Of course, Miss Catherine was desperate with worry.

"I shan't feel happy until I've seen him, Nelly. I must tell Linton that it's not my fault I haven't written, and I must convince him there's no hope for the two of us."

I tried my best to change her mind, but she was determined to go, and the very next morning we set out for Wuthering Heights. I hoped young Linton would be so uninterested in her that Catherine would see immediately that Heathcliff was lying.

We found Linton on his own, sitting in a chair by the fire and looking very weak and ill. Catherine raced towards him.

"Is that you, Catherine?" he said, slowly raising his head. "No – don't kiss me, it takes my breath away. Father said you would call. Would you shut the door? I hate being cold."

"Well, Linton," Catherine began, when she had closed the door and he had stopped frowning. "Aren't you pleased to see me?"

"Why didn't you come before?" he answered peevishly. "You should have come then, instead of writing. It wore me out writing those long letters. And now I'm too tired to do anything at all."

Catherine asked Linton anxiously what she could do to help and, while she was pouring him a drink, her cousin continued, "Father told me you stopped writing because you despised me."

"No, I don't despise you, Linton! After papa and Nelly, I love you better than anyone else in the world."

"And will you come and visit me again?"

"Of course," said Catherine, stroking his long, soft hair. "If only papa would allow it, I'd spend half my time with you. Pretty Linton! I wish you were my brother, then we could be together all the time."

"But father says that if you were my wife you'd love me better than anyone else in the world, and that's what I want."

"I could never love anyone more than papa,"

Catherine said seriously. "You know that sometimes men can hate their wives. Papa told me your father hated your mother and that's why she left him."

"That's not true," said the boy. "And anyway, your mother hated your father, and she loved mine!"

"You little liar! I hate you now!" Catherine snapped, her face red with fury.

"She did! She did!" shouted out Linton, leaning forward to see if she would cry.

Catherine gave her cousin's chair a violent push, and he fell backwards, coughing violently. His coughing fit lasted so long that even I was frightened, and Catherine was terrified that she had really hurt him. But at last he recovered.

"How do you feel now, Linton?" she asked anxiously. "I'm so sorry I hurt you. I thought it was only a little push. Don't let me go home thinking I've hurt you."

"I can't speak to you now," he sulked. "You've hurt me so much I'll lie awake all night choking with this cough. And I was feeling better before you came!"

"Come, Miss Catherine," I said, trying to hurry her away. "You can see Linton isn't dying of love for you. And there's nothing you can do to make him feel better. So come with me and we'll leave him to sleep."

I had a very hard time persuading her to leave. And I was alarmed to see, just before we left, that she was whispering something in Linton's ear.

On our way home, I told Catherine she must never see Linton again, but she only smiled at me.

"The Grange is not a prison, Nelly, and you are not my jailer. And, besides, I'm almost seventeen years old. I'm sure that Linton would recover if I was looking after him. He's a pretty little darling when he's good, and I'd make such a pet of him that we would never quarrel."

I frowned to hear this.

"Don't you like him, Nelly?"

"Like him!" I exclaimed. "He's the most selfish boy I've ever met, and I don't think he'll live until he's twenty. I'm pleased you won't be marrying him. And if you've any ideas of visiting Wuthering Heights again, I'll tell your father, and you know what that would do to him!"

I must have caught a cold on our walk to the Heights, because the next day I was forced to stay in bed. For three weeks I didn't leave my room and during that time Catherine behaved like an angel, dividing her days between her father's room and mine. But I never thought to ask myself what she did in the evenings. Sometimes, I noticed that her cheeks looked very pink when she came to say goodnight to me, but I thought she had been sitting by the fire.

On the first day that I was up again, I asked Miss Catherine to keep me company after tea, but she was very restless. Eventually, she told me she was ill and went off to bed early. Later that evening, I went up to her room and discovered it was empty! So I sat in the dark, waiting for her to return.

At last, Catherine crept in silently. She was just

shaking the snow off her clothes when I stood up.

"Miss Catherine!" I said, more sad than angry. "Why you have been deceiving me? And how long has this been going on?"

Soon, she had told me the whole story. For the past three weeks she had been riding over to Wuthering Heights every night. She and Linton had spent every evening together. Sometimes they had been happy, when he made an effort to be less selfish, but most of the time she had been miserable. But, in spite of his difficult moods, Catherine insisted she must keep visiting her cousin – he needed her so badly, and she wanted to make him happy. She tried to make me promise not to tell her father, but I knew that things had gone too far.

I went straight to Mr. Edgar's study and told him all I knew. He was shocked and upset, and the next morning he told Catherine she must never visit the Heights again. Nothing she could say would make her father change his mind, and she knew she had to obey him, even though it made her very sad.

A few days later, my master asked me to tell him truthfully what I thought of young Linton.

"He's very delicate, sir," I replied, "and he can be selfish, but he isn't like his father. I don't think he is thoroughly wicked."

Edgar sighed and looked out towards the churchyard.

"I've often prayed for death, Nelly, so that I can join my beloved Cathy again. But now I'm afraid of what will happen to Catherine. Young Linton will inherit the Grange when I'm dead, and then where will she live? Perhaps it would be best if Catherine married him."

"All we can do is wait and see what happens," was the best answer I could give.

Spring arrived, and Mr. Edgar was no better. I could see he was desperately worried about Miss Catherine's future and, in the end, he decided to do something about it. So he wrote a letter to Linton inviting him to the Grange. The boy replied immediately, saying his father would not allow him to visit the Grange, but perhaps he could meet his cousin for a ride? Edgar was very unhappy about this, because he wasn't strong enough to accompany his daughter. But after some more letters from Linton – most of which I'm sure were written by Heathcliff – Edgar at last agreed to a meeting.

It was summer by the time Catherine and I set out on our first ride to meet her cousin. We had arranged to meet at the edge of Thrushcross Park, but then a messenger arrived to tell us Master Linton was up on the moors. I was very worried about this change of plan, and I became even more concerned when I saw the state he was in. Linton was lying back on the heather, struggling to breathe. Catherine looked at him in horror.

"Oh Linton, are you very ill? You seem so much worse."

"No, I'm better. Really, I'm better," he insisted.

But his large blue eyes filled with tears.

Catherine tried her best to comfort him, but he didn't seem to want to talk to her at all, and he kept glancing fearfully back at the Heights.

"I think you should go home," Catherine told her cousin. "I can see my tales and chatter don't amuse you any more."

This suggestion made Linton very agitated and he clasped her hand, begging her not to go. "Please stay for another half an hour," he pleaded. "My father will

be so angry with me if you go."

I immediately suspected some plot of Heathcliff's and wanted to leave immediately. But Catherine agreed to stay a little longer, and she sat beside her cousin while he dozed and whimpered. Before we left, Linton made Catherine promise to meet him again at the same place in a week's time.

We rode back to the Grange together, troubled and unhappy. I advised Miss Catherine to tell her father as little as possible about our meeting – he was now very ill, and I didn't want to worry him with news about his nephew.

Each day that week, Edgar became noticeably weaker. Catherine realized that her father was dying and spent all the time she could by his bedside. By Thursday, she was looking very strained and pale, and I thought that another ride on the moors might do her some good. Mr. Edgar was happy to let Catherine meet her cousin. He had no idea how ill Linton was.

Linton was lying in the same place on the moors, but this time he was even more feverish and frightened.

"I thought you weren't coming!" he said angrily.

"Why don't you be honest and say you don't want to see me?" Catherine replied. "My father is very ill and I ought to be with him."

Linton began to sob with fear. "Catherine, please don't leave me. My life is in your hands. I can't explain, but if you leave me now, my father would kill me. Please agree to what he says and then perhaps he won't hurt me."

Catherine weakened. "Agree to what?" she asked. "You've got to explain to me, Linton."

At that moment, I heard a rustle in the heather, and I looked up to see Heathcliff striding over the moors.

"Greetings, Nelly!" he cried out heartily. "How are things at the Grange? Is it true that Edgar Linton is dying?"

"Yes, it is true."

"How long will he last, do you think?" he asked urgently. "That boy over there is dying too, and I'd thank his uncle to be quick or Linton will die before him and all my plans will be ruined."

He looked over to where Linton was lying on the grass. "Get up, boy!" he shouted angrily to his son, who flinched away from him. Then he turned to Catherine. "Would you be so kind as to walk home with Linton? The cowardly wretch shudders whenever I touch him."

"Linton dear," said Catherine, "you know I can't go to Wuthering Heights – papa has forbidden it."

"Well, then the boy will have to come with me," roared Heathcliff, making a grab for him.

"No, no!" screamed Linton, terrified of what Heathcliff might do to him on their return. "Catherine, you must help me. Come with me please!"

In the end, Catherine simply couldn't refuse, so we all walked back to the Heights together, Linton leaning heavily on his young cousin's arm.

As soon as we were inside the house, Heathcliff turned the key in the lock, and I realized with a sinking heart that we were trapped.

"All the servants are out today," he said calmly, "so we are quite alone."

"Give me that key," cried Catherine, her eyes flashing. "I won't stay here and I'm not afraid of you!"

Heathcliff held the key firmly in his fist but she attacked it with her nails and then with her teeth. The next minute, he struck her violently on the side of the face and she staggered back, trembling.

"Now, young lady," Heathcliff said grimly, "you'll do as I tell you. I'll be your father tomorrow and I'll punish you every day if I see that temper in your eyes again!" Then Heathcliff went out into the yard, locking the door behind him.

Catherine and I raced around the kitchen, trying to find a way to escape, but all the doors and windows were locked. Meanwhile, Linton had settled himself comfortably into a chair, happy to see someone else in trouble. I threatened him with a slapping if he didn't explain his father's plans, and he soon poured out the whole story to us.

"Father wants Catherine to marry me, so he has control over her as well. But he's afraid that I'm going to die, so we have to do it tomorrow. You have to stay here all night, and marry me in the morning."

"Marry you!" I exclaimed. "The man must be insane! Why should a beautiful, healthy girl like

Catherine tie herself to a pathetic creature like you."

I couldn't resist giving him a shaking, and that started a terrible coughing fit.

"I must get out of here tonight, if I have to burn down the door," said Catherine desperately. "I love my father more than you, Linton, and I have to see him now."

At that moment, Heathcliff returned, having let our horses loose to run over the moors. He ordered Linton to go to bed immediately and turned to us.

"Mr. Heathcliff," Catherine began bravely, "I must go home now or papa will be miserable. But I promise you I will marry your son. Papa would like me to and I love Linton. So why do you need to force me to do something I'll do willingly?"

"Well, Miss Linton," said the villain, "I'm delighted to hear that your father will be miserable – that's certainly made up my mind to keep you here overnight. And I'll make sure you don't leave Wuthering Heights until you've kept your promise to marry Linton."

"Then please send Nelly to tell my father that I'm all right!" sobbed Catherine bitterly. "Poor papa will think we are lost!"

"I won't do anything to make that man happy," growled Heathcliff, "and I'll be glad to see you miserable too. I've taught Linton to be a selfish and cruel husband, and I shall enjoy watching you suffer!"

Then Heathcliff dragged us both upstairs to the housekeeper's room and locked us in. Neither of us slept at all that night. Catherine stood for hours by the window, gazing out over the moors, and I spent a terrible night, blaming myself for everything that had happened.

At seven o'clock the next morning, Heathcliff came and took Catherine away, and I was left alone. For the next four days, I was kept locked up. The only person I saw was Hareton, who delivered my meals in silence, obviously obeying Heathcliff's orders.

On the fifth day, Zillah came into my room. She was amazed to see me there – everyone had thought that Catherine and I had lost our way on the moors and died out there. I rushed straight out of the room and searched the house for Catherine, but I couldn't find her anywhere. But I did find Linton, lying on a sofa and sucking a stick of candy.

"Where's Miss Catherine?" I demanded sternly.

"She's locked up in a room upstairs," he replied calmly. "We won't let her go yet. Father says I mustn't be soft on her. He says she hates me and wants me to die. So now I'm punishing her. She can cry as much as she likes, I won't let her go home."

And he went back to sucking his candy stick.

"Master Heathcliff," I said angrily, "have you forgotten Miss Catherine's kindness to you when she came to visit you last winter? Think of all the times she rode through wind and snow to see you. And now you're believing the lies your father tells you, and turning against her. What a spoiled, selfish boy you are!"

"I'm tired of her crying," Linton answered crossly. "She gives me a headache. She promised me that if I gave her the key to her room she'd give me all her books from the Grange, but I told her that they weren't hers to give and I would inherit them all when her father died. So then she offered me her locket with the pictures of her mother and father, but I said that was mine as well and tried to snatch it from her.

"Then she pushed me away and hurt me so much I screamed and father came in to see what was happening. He hit her on the face and knocked her down. Then he crushed the locket under his foot and took away the picture of her mother."

"And were you pleased to see her hurt?" I asked.

"I was pleased that father punished her. But I didn't like to see her mouth full of blood. She hasn't said a word to me since then. I think she shouldn't cry so much – she looks so pale and wild she frightens me."

I saw there was no chance of persuading Linton to help me, so I decided to run back to the Grange as fast as I could, and then try to rescue Catherine later.

Everyone at the Grange was delighted to see me – and relieved to hear that my mistress was still alive. I hurried up to Mr. Edgar's room to give him the news and was horrified to see how much he had changed. It was clear he couldn't last much longer.

"Catherine," he murmured, as he heard me walk over to him.

I touched his hand. "Catherine is coming, dear master!" I whispered. "She's alive and well, and I hope she will be here tonight."

He half rose up, and looked eagerly around the room, but then he sank back again. I told him as much as I dared about what had happened up at the Heights.

Mr. Edgar gave orders for four servants to go up to the Heights and bring back his daughter immediately. They were gone for hours, but eventually they returned without her – Heathcliff had frightened them away. I began to be afraid that Mr. Edgar would never see Catherine again, when I heard a noise at the door. It was my brave mistress, who had managed to escape from the Heights. And she ran, sobbing, into my arms.

"Nelly! Nelly! Is papa still alive?"

"Yes, he is, my angel," I cried. "Thank God you're safe with us again!"

She wanted to run straight up to her father's room, but I made her sit quietly and catch her breath. I begged her to tell her father that she was happy with Linton, so he could die peacefully, and she promised me that she would.

I stood outside the bedroom door and heard Edgar and Catherine talking quietly together. Everything was calm. Catherine kept her despair to herself and her father died a happy man. Kissing his daughter's cheek, he murmured, "I am going to be with Cathy now, and one day you, my darling child, shall come and join us too!"

Heathcliff allowed Catherine to stay at the Grange until the day of Mr. Edgar's funeral, but that evening he came to take her back to the Heights. I begged him to let her stay at the Grange and send Linton to live with us, but he refused.

"I'm looking for a tenant for Thrushcross Grange," he answered, "and I want my children near me. Besides, I'm going to make sure that Catherine works for her living."

"I shall work," said Catherine, bravely. "And I shall look after Linton, because he's the only person I have to love in the world. But you, Heathcliff, have no one to love you, and nobody to cry for you when you die!"

"Don't you talk to me like that, you little witch," said her new father-in-law grimly. "Now go off and get your things."

While Catherine was gone, Heathcliff looked around the room, and took down the portrait of Cathy to keep for himself.

"Do you have any idea, Nelly, how Cathy has

haunted me over the years?" he said. "Every time I leave my house, she's waiting for me on the moors, and whenever I come home I see her at the door. I tried sleeping in her room for a while, but it was pure torment. She was always there, crying to be let in, but as soon as I opened the window she was gone. She's been teasing me like that for eighteen years – killing me by inches until I'm insane with grief!"

After a while, Miss Catherine came in, ready for her journey. When she kissed me goodbye, her lips felt like ice.

"Come and see me soon, Nelly. Please don't forget."

"You'll do no such thing!" thundered Heathcliff. "I'll have no more prying in my house!"

I watched the two of them walk away with a very heavy heart.

Since Miss Catherine left the Grange, almost a year ago, I have never seen her face. But Zillah, the housekeeper, has given me some news. I believe that Catherine tried her hardest to look after her husband. Heathcliff refused to call a doctor, and Linton only lasted a few weeks after their marriage. In the end, he died in agony, with only Catherine by his side. Heathcliff inherited all his son's property and Catherine has nothing of her own.

It must be so lonely for my dear Catherine up at Wuthering Heights. Joseph and Zillah won't talk to her because they think that she's too proud, and Heathcliff despises her. Only Hareton shows her any kindness, but she takes no notice of him because he's so rough and uneducated. What would make me happiest of all would be to rent a little cottage and live with Miss Catherine again, but I know that Heathcliff would never allow it.

That was the sad end of Nelly Dean's story. After weeks of listening to her memories, I wanted to leave the moors and return to my life in London again. So I decided to ride over to Wuthering Heights the very next day and tell my landlord about my plans. I certainly don't intend to spend another winter in this wild and desolate place.

Return to the Heights

The weather was frosty but bright when I rode up to Wuthering Heights, carrying a note from Nelly for young Mrs. Heathcliff. Hareton Earnshaw opened the door and I had a good look at him – he was certainly the most handsome farm worker I'd ever seen. I thought he looked intelligent and kind, in spite of the way that Heathcliff had treated him.

Hareton led me into the kitchen, where Catherine was busy chopping up vegetables. She didn't even bother to look up when I came in.

"Well," I thought to myself, "she may be beautiful, but she's certainly no angel."

As I passed Catherine's chair, I dropped Nelly's note in front of her, but Hareton had noticed it and grabbed it up quickly.

"Mr. Heathcliff will want to look at this," he said, stuffing it into his pocket. But then Catherine started to cry. As soon as he saw her tears, Hareton weakened and passed the letter over to her. It was obvious he couldn't bear to make her sad.

Catherine read through the letter several times, and asked me many questions about life at the Grange. "Please tell Nelly," she said, "that I would love to answer her letter, but I have no paper and pencils. Heathcliff has taken everything away from me – even my books."

"No books!" I exclaimed. "How do you manage to live here without anything to read?"

"I used to read all the time but, when Heathcliff realized my books made me happy, he took them away from me. I've searched all over the house for them but they've gone – all except a few in Hareton's room. But I can't see why he needs them because he's such a dunce he can't even read!"

Hareton blushed crimson and I decided to come to his rescue.

"Perhaps he is learning to read?" I suggested.

"Well, he has a lot to learn," said Catherine scornfully. "You should hear the stupid mistakes he makes – they make me want to laugh out loud!"

146

Hareton took a deep breath and left the room. In a few minutes he was back again with a pile of books, which he threw on the floor. "Why don't you take them now?" he said, pale with rage. "I never want to see them again!"

"Well I don't want them either," Catherine replied spitefully. "I hate them now because they make me think of you."

Hareton gathered up the books and threw them into the fire. Then he stormed out of the room.

As Hareton left the kitchen, Heathcliff arrived. He seemed moody and restless, and he was much thinner than the last time I had seen him.

"I've come to tell you that I'm leaving the Grange," I announced. "I'll pay the rest of my rent, but I'll be gone within a few days."

"So, Mr. Lockwood, you're tired of the moors already," Heathcliff replied. "But stay and have lunch with us before you go. A guest who is not in danger of coming again is always welcome here."

So Heathcliff, Hareton and I sat down to lunch in the sitting room, while Catherine was banished to the kitchen to eat with the servants. It was not a cheerful meal. Heathcliff was grim and surly, and Hareton was completely silent. As soon as it was over I set out for the Grange. I was happy to think I would never see Wuthering Heights again.

I had been away from Thrushcross Grange for six months when I happened to be passing through

Yorkshire once more. I wasn't in a hurry, so I decided to stay the night at Gimmerton, and visit my old housekeeper and friend, Nelly Dean. But when I arrived at the Grange, a strange woman opened the door. She told me Nelly had moved up to the Heights, so I set off once more on the familiar path across the moors.

As I approached the Heights, I was surprised to see flowers growing in the garden. The doors and windows were wide open and I could see two young people inside, sitting at a table.

"Now read it again," said a voice as sweet as a bell, "and this time get it right, or I'll pull your hair!"

"I'll try one more time," answered a deep voice, "but you must kiss me if I get it right."

Then the young man began to read. His handsome features glowed with pleasure, and his eyes kept wandering from the page to a small white hand resting on his knee. I watched while he finished the passage and claimed his reward from his beautiful teacher. Then I left them and went to find Nelly.

I soon found my old friend sewing in the kitchen. She was delighted to see me.

"But why have you moved to Wuthering Heights, Nelly?" I asked. "And where is your master, Mr. Heathcliff?"

"Oh, he's dead, sir," she replied. "He died three months ago."

"Heathcliff dead!" I couldn't believe it. "But tell me, Nelly, how did it happen?"

The good woman fetched me a drink and then settled down to her story...

A few weeks after you left us, I was summoned to the Heights. It seemed that Heathcliff hated the sight of Catherine – I think she reminded him too much of her mother – so he wanted me to keep her away from him. We were given a small room at the back of the house and I brought a great number of books with me to keep her amused. At first, Catherine was happy just to be with me, but then she grew restless in her prison. Heathcliff wouldn't even allow her to walk in the garden and she hated being indoors all day. Apart from me, her only companion was Hareton, who often came to sit with us. But I don't know how he stood it, because Catherine teased him terribly for being so dull and stupid.

Then, one day, Catherine decided to be friendly to Hareton. She apologized to her cousin for treating him so badly, and worked out a clever way of helping him to read. Each day, she read to him from one of her books but, just as the story was becoming really exciting, she deliberately broke off and left him longing to read the rest. Then she helped him to stumble over the sentences until he had finished the story for himself.

I can't say that Catherine is a patient teacher and Hareton has a great deal to learn, but each day he improves and the two of them grow closer and closer. Now, when I see them together it's like a dream come true, and I'll be the happiest woman in England on the day that they get married!

But I must get back to my story...

At first, Heathcliff didn't realize what was happening to the cousins, but then one lunchtime old Joseph rushed into the kitchen.

"Now look what that little fiend has made the boy do!" he roared. "He's pulled up my fruit bushes to plant her stupid flowers!"

"Hareton, can you explain yourself?" asked Heathcliff.

But Catherine interrupted. "It was my fault," she

admitted bravely. "I asked him to do it. I thought it would be nice to have some flowers there."

"And who gave you permission for that?" growled Heathcliff.

"I think you should let us have a piece of garden for ourselves. After all, you've stolen all my land and Hareton's too! He and I are friends now, and you can't treat us badly any longer."

Heathcliff turned very pale and stood up suddenly, staring at her.

"If you hit me, Hareton will hit you back," she said, "and he's just as strong as you. He won't obey you any more. Soon he'll hate you as much as I do."

"Please stop, Catherine," muttered Hareton. "I don't want to quarrel with Heathcliff."

But it was too late. Heathcliff had grabbed Catherine by the arm, his eyes flashing like a wild beast's, ready to tear her to pieces. Catherine stared back at him defiantly, and I was just about to try rescuing her when Heathcliff's fingers suddenly relaxed, and he gazed intently into her face as if he had seen a ghost. Then he drew his hand over his eyes and stood still as a stone.

"You must learn not to make me angry," he said in a quiet, shaken voice, "or I'll end up murdering you. Now, go away all of you, and leave me alone!"

Then he went out and didn't come back until very late.

When Heathcliff returned, the cousins were sitting side by side, looking at a book. As he came into the kitchen, they looked up at him together with the same dark eyes – eyes which were just like Cathy Earnshaw's – and I saw Heathcliff give a deep sigh. Then they escaped into the garden and I was left alone with him.

"This is a ridiculous end, don't you think, Nelly?" he observed. "I've worked all my life to destroy the Earnshaws and the Lintons. I've won all their money and their land, but now that I have them completely in my power, I no longer care about my revenge. What's the use of destroying them now?"

Heathcliff paced around the room. "Something is happening to me, Nelly. I can feel a strange change coming in my life, and its shadow is hanging over me. I'm not interested in living any more – I can hardly even remember to eat or drink. I hate to see Catherine and Hareton because they remind me so much of Cathy. But then – everything I see reminds me of her! I see her in every cloud and tree. Wherever I go, I'm surrounded by her."

"What do you mean by a change?" I said. "You're not ill, are you, sir?"

"No, I'm not ill, Nelly. In fact, I'm ridiculously strong. But I no longer want to live. I can't carry on like this. I have to remind myself to breathe – almost remind my heart to beat! I have just one wish that I've wanted for so long. It's a long fight, and I wish that it could be over!"

Then he began to pace around the room again, muttering terrible things to himself.

After that day, we hardly saw Heathcliff. He

stopped eating meals with us and spent most of his time out on the moors. Sometimes he stayed out all night, and when he came home in the morning he was smiling and shivering, as if he was possessed by a strange, wild happiness. There were times when he would stop breathing for as much as half a minute. Then he would gaze into the distance with glittering, restless eyes, as though he was looking at something the rest of us couldn't see.

After a few weeks of wanderings, Heathcliff locked himself in Cathy's old room. He spent most of his days and nights in there, but from the terrible moans that I heard, I don't think he slept at all. One evening, he came downstairs, looking gaunt and wild, and began pacing up and down in front of the fire. I begged him to rest and have something to eat, but it was no use.

"Nelly," he said desperately, "you can't stop me now. I've been in hell for eighteen years, and now at last I'm in sight of my heaven. I can see it waiting for me!

"I can't rest now, Nelly, although I'm so tired. You may as well tell a man who's struggling through the sea to rest within an arm's length of the shore! I must reach it first, and then I'll rest. So keep well away from me now, Nelly! So long as you keep away, you'll see nothing to frighten you."

I obeyed my master's orders and stayed away from his room all day, trying hard to ignore his terrible sobs and groans. But the next day, when he still didn't appear, I sent Hareton to the village to fetch Doctor Kenneth. When the doctor arrived, though, Heathcliff refused to unlock his door and shouted out so fiercely that he went away again.

That night was very stormy and wet, and when I walked through the garden the next morning, I was surprised to see the window of Cathy's old room swinging wide open. "If Heathcliff is in bed," I thought to myself, "he'll be drenched right through."

I decided I had to open the door, whatever my master said, so I took a bunch of keys and tried them all until I found the one that worked.

Heathcliff was lying on the bed, his eyes wide open and staring, and it seemed that he was smiling at me! His face and clothes were dripping with rain and he was completely still. When I stretched out my hand to touch him, he was as cold as ice. There was no doubt that Heathcliff was dead.

I fastened the window and combed my master's long, black hair away from his forehead. Then I tried to close his eyes, but they wouldn't stay shut. I cried out for Joseph, but the old man refused to touch the body.

"See, the devil has taken his soul," he cried. "Look how wicked he is, smiling at death!" Then he sank down on his knees to pray.

Hareton was very sad about Heathcliff's death, even though he had treated him so badly, but no one else mourned for him at all. On the day of Heathcliff's funeral, only Hareton and I were there to watch him buried next to his beloved Cathy, just as he had wished.

At this point, Nelly stopped her story, and her face broke into a smile. "The next time I go to Gimmerton Church, Mr. Lockwood, it will be for a much more cheerful occasion. Hareton and Catherine will be married on New Year's Day, and then they will go to live at Thrushcross Grange."

"So what will happen to Wuthering Heights?" I asked.

"Old Joseph will stay on there, and live in the kitchen, but the rest of the house will be shut up, and left to its ghosts."

On my way back to Gimmerton, I walked through the churchyard, looking for three stones. They were easy to find, standing together in the corner of the graveyard, close to the edge of the moor. Cathy's stone was half buried in plants and moss, and some plants were starting to creep over Edgar's grave beside it. But Heathcliff's stone, on the other side of Cathy's, was still bare and new.

Some people say that they have seen the ghosts of Cathy and Heathcliff, wandering hand-in-hand over the moors. But I would like to think that they are now at peace. I stayed by their graves for a long while on that beautiful summer's evening, watching the butterflies flutter though the heather and listening to the wind breathe softly through the grass. And I imagined the sleepers resting peacefully at last, silent and still under that quiet earth.

Other versions
of the story

The dramatic story of *Wuthering Heights* has been adapted many times. It has been turned into musicals, plays, movies, and even a ballet and an opera. American, British, Spanish, French and Japanese film directors have all made their own versions of Emily Brontë's classic novel. The story has even inspired a pop song – in 1978, British singer Kate Bush recorded a haunting lament in the voice of the ghostly Cathy, which went straight to the top of the charts.

The most famous film version of *Wuthering Heights* was made in 1939. Produced by Samuel Goldwyn in black and white, it is considered a cinema classic and presents a very romantic story, with Lawrence Olivier as a wild, demon-possessed Heathcliff and Merle Oberon as a proud and headstrong Cathy. Although it was filmed entirely in Hollywood, Goldwyn's *Wuthering Heights* manages to convey a sense of the menacing wildness of the Yorkshire moors. But the Californian sunshine made the heather grow to knee-height – something it would never have done in Yorkshire!

A much less sentimental adaptation of Emily Brontë's novel appeared in 1971, starring Timothy Dalton as Heathcliff and Anna Calder-Marshall as Cathy. Director Robert Fuest filmed most of his scenes on the Yorkshire moors and was not afraid to include some of the novel's more brutal scenes. But, like Samuel Goldwyn, he only tells half of Emily Brontë's story, completely cutting out the second generation of characters.

The most faithful film version of the novel was directed in 1993 by Peter Kosminsky. It tells the whole story of Wuthering Heights, with Juliet Binoche playing the double part of Cathy and her daughter Catherine. Ralph Fiennes plays Heathcliff as a tormented and savage outsider, and some of the characters' speeches are taken straight from the novel.

Another Usborne Classic

Jane Eyre

FROM THE STORY BY
CHARLOTTE BRONTË

Suddenly, a terrible, savage scream ripped the night apart. It echoed the length of Thornfield Hall, then died away, leaving me fixed to the spot.

The scream had come from above and, sure enough, as I listened, I heard the sounds of a struggle in an attic room upstairs. Then a muffled man's voice shouted: "Help! Help! Help!"

A poor orphan, Jane Eyre is bullied by her rich relations and sent away to school. Determined to change her luck, she becomes a governess and settles happily into a new life at Thornfield Hall. But why is Mr. Rochester, her employer, so mysterious, and whose menacing laugh does Jane keep hearing at night?